The Online Date

Betty Brooks

The Online Date

By

Betty Brooks

DEDICATION

I dedicate this book to all the men and women who have learned the art of love and what it means to experience all of the smiles and frowns, joys and sadness, sweetness and bitterness, learning the true essence of what love really is, which is what you and your partner paint it to be.

ACKNOWLEDGMENTS

I would like to acknowledge God, who first and
foremost makes all things possible.
I would also like to acknowledge my daughter,
Patience, who edits, typesets, proofreads, does the
interior, covers, and put this book together.
My wonderful and smart daughter you are awesome.
Simply awesome.
My son, Luke, you supported me to no end. I love
you dearly.

1

The Online Date

"Girl, I need to tell you something, but let me finish talking before you say anything."

"Oohkay," Anna said, hesitantly.

Five seconds passed and Lola had not said a word.

"Of course, I am going to scream if you don't tell me what it is."

Lola closed her eyes and took a quick deep breath and exhaled slowly. She knew Anna was not going to like what she had to tell her, but knew it was time. Smiling, she opened her eyes.

"For goodness sake, Lola, what is it?"

"I have been seeing someone."

"You mean seeing someone...like a man?"

Lola bobbed her head up and down in the affirmative.

"Well, it is about time. I thought you were never going to meet somebody," Anna said, clapping her hands.

"Okay, girl, fess' up. When, where and how long?"

Before Lola could answer her, Anna shook her finger at Lola, "You have been holding out on me. Girl, come on, talk to me."

Lola pushed the words through her lips as fast as she could get them out.

"His name is Hunter and we met online."

"You what!" Anna exclaimed.

"Oh, Lola nooo! Girl, please tell me you didn't."

"Anna, please. Just hear me out…" Anna stopped Lola in mid-sentence.

"Oh, Lola! No. Noo!" Anna continued to wail.

"You know we agreed to never date online. That is bad news. Bad, bad news."

Eyeing her friend of six years suspiciously, Anna asked, "How long have you been talking with him?"

"About five and a half weeks, closer to six."

"And you never thought to tell me?"

"Well. There was nothing to tell. Until now. Come on, Anna, it's no big deal. We've been talking on the phone, skyping a little and we did one zoom call."

"I honestly thought he would have lost interest by now. But, instead he wants to meet me. Take me to dinner."

"I am telling you so you and Sam can maybe sit across from us at the restaurant and check him out. You know. Make sure he doesn't kidnap me or something worse."

"Oh, Lola," Anna sighed, "I don't like it."

"Come on, Anna. Hunter seems very nice."

Anna rolled her eyes to the ceiling, shaking her head negatively.

"They all do…at first. Treat you like gold, platinum and silver…the works. That is until they get their hooks in you."

"Look, we are going to be in a public place," Lola explained.

"At least give me some credit for good common sense. Of course I want to date a good man, get to know him, get married someday with a home and two, maybe three children, but not at the expense of my life. That being said, how will I know one way or the other, if I never give him a chance?" Lola continued.

"Well, I still don't like it, "Anna said, grudgingly.

"I just need to know that you have my back. I am paying for your dinner if you come," she explained to Anna.

"If Sam agrees to come along, he can pay for his own dinner."

"Of course I have your back, Lola. I just don't want you to get hurt."

"I am not going to get hurt. Trust me. My heart is guarded better than Fort Knox."

"Well I certainly hope so. Just don't forget what happened to me two years ago. I mean, I almost got killed. My online date was a Psycho from hell."

"Yeah right," Lola said.

"I almost lost my best friend. Of course, a lot of what happened to you could have been avoided if you had only listened to your friends and been more careful."

"Don't be hating," Anna said, not smiling.

"You know y'all could have given me more support with Frank. I thought we were doing just fine until y'all made him angry."

"We did not make him angry or mad. He knew we had caught him cheating on you and when we told you and you confronted him he blew up."

"Goodness, Anna, you paid for everything y'all did. Dinners, outings when we were together, vacations. For God sake, Anna, you let the man sleep over some nights...after only one week of knowing him. We asked you not to confront him alone about his affairs with women, but you didn't listen."

"Soo," Lola continued unapologetically, "if you want to blame us for Frank almost killing you then go right ahead. If that's what floats your boat that is all well and good, but your friends are not the one who was one inch from death's door."

Lola put her hands on her hips and stared at Anna seriously and said, "And did you ever notice the way he would look at me? I still get chills when I think about it."

Sighing heavily, Anna told Lola she was right.

"That is why I want you to be careful. If I don't like him you are not going out with him again," Anna said, seriously.

"Just pay attention to him at dinner," Lola continued.

"I won't look your way during dinner. However, if I drop my napkin, call me on my phone with some emergency excuse to leave right away."

"Girl you know I got your back."

Staring at her friend, Anna asked, "When is this dinner going to take place?"

"Friday night at seven thirty." Raising her eyebrows at Anna and smiling, Lola said, "Guess where he wants to take me?"

"You know I don't like guessing games, Lola, so please just tell me."

"Sometimes, Anna, you are no fun. Okay," she said, still smiling, "he is taking me to 'The Chopanique'."

"Isn't that a whole lot of fancy for a first time date that might not work?" Anna said, dryly.

"I know right. And when I mentioned it, he said I was worth it. I asked him if I could choose a less expensive place and he said and I quote, "you can choose on our next date." end quote."

"Well, the jury is still out on him for now. No wonder you offered to pay for my meal. The place is uba expensive, but not to worry, I will pay for my meal. I am not broke, you know."

"As a matter of fact, I am ready to meet this 'trying to show off guy'. This date will probably set him back two whole weeks of his paycheck. Maybe three depending on where he works."

"Anna, will you stop trying to put the man down? All our black men are not trying to live off wealthy black women. I won't prejudge the man before I even know him."

"I wouldn't call it prejudging. I call it common sense. Now let's get back to work so we can go shopping and find you a hot dress for your fancy date."

"Girl, please," Lola said, wiping her lips for crumbs before getting up from the lunch table.

"I am not buying a new dress for a date I don't even know is going to last," Lola continued, laughing as they headed back to work.

"Has traffic always been this bad?" Anna asked when she was unable to get off at their exit.

"Around lunch time, yeah. The next exit will get us back to work on time," Lola said.

"You're right, but I still think people are moving here by the dozens every week. Everywhere is getting more crowded. And housing is ridiculous. Everything is going up."

"Are you having problems with money? If so, you know I got your back," Lola was saying when Anna cut her off.

"No, Lola. I am not having money problems. I think I am venting because of your date. I am worried about you."

"Anna, I thank you for having my back, but girl it is just a date. Please give it a rest. Stop all this negative talking. You're making me nervous."

"Maybe you should be nervous," Anna said under her breath.

"I heard that," Lola said, humorously.

In the elevator at work Lola got off on the second floor. "Talk to you later," Lola said happily.

"Okay. We will talk after work," Anna said as the doors closed and continued to the fifth floor.

"Looks like someone has an admirer," Pam said, pointing to Lola's office door.

"What?" Lola asked.

"You will see," her secretary told her, smiling.

Lola stopped mid stride when she looked at her desk. Sitting on her desk were five of the most beautiful red roses she had ever seen surrounded by white baby breaths.

She quickly pulled the card from them. After reading the card, she held it to her heart, took a deep breath, smiled and slowly exhaled.

Picking up the phone with shaky fingers, she pressed a button. "Get down here to my office now!"

"Lola, is everything alright?"

"Now, Anna!" Lola said without answering her.

In record time Anna rushed into Lola's office.

"Lola what's wrong? Did something happen to your mom?"

Shaking her head negatively she gave the card to Anna.

"So mister date guy is at it again, ha," Anna said dryly.

"What do you mean?" Lola asked, hating she called Anna to her office.

"Come on, Lola. Girl, wake up and get your head out the sand. This man is setting you up for the biggest sex orgy there is," Anna said, too loudly.

"Please lower your voice," Lola whispered loudly, closing her door. "People can hear you. My boss works on this floor."

Lowering her voice, Anna continued.

"Listen to me, Lola. As a friend, I am warning you. This man wants to get in your pants. No man is going to spend that much money on you and not want something in return."

"Anna, every man is not like Frank. Frank was a man that preyed on women who had money. Goodness, Anna."

"You live in a four bedroom home with enough amenities to satisfy the rich and famous…and you brought him to your home the first week."

"Oh," Anna said, meanly, "so now you're an expert on men all of a sudden. I mean, how did Hunter, if that's even his real name, know where you work? I am telling you, Lola…leave that man now before your heart gets involved."

"You know what, Anna. You can leave now. I thought you would be a little happy for me."

Lola could feel a migraine coming on and she knew first hand they were no joke. Rubbing her temples, she couldn't believe her friend would be so unbending.

"As a matter of fact, don't come to dinner on Friday night. You are way too negative. I don't need that negative energy anywhere near me."

"Goodness, Anna, Frank put two ladies in the hospital before you met him. One is paralyzed in one arm from the stab wounds he gave her. The other woman he kidnapped for two days before she was found."

"Frank was no good. He was rotten to the core. I'm not going into this relationship with Hunter blind and ignorant. I am going to be careful. Believe me!" she reiterated, "Hunter definitely did not come to my house the first week…or the second…not even the third. And I am definitely not going to start paying for everything we do. "

"All right, Lola. I got it. You don't have to be so mean about it. And I won't come to dinner, either. But don't say I didn't warn you," Anna said and stormed out the door.

"Are you alright Ms. Wells?" Pam asked, walking into Lola's office after Anna stormed past her desk.

"Yeah. I'm okay. I just thought a friend…my best friend, would want to share in my happiness. I keep telling her I am going to be careful, but she won't listen. I mean, I'm not stupid."

Correctly understanding what happened, Pam walked to the side cabinet, opened a drawer, took out a small container, went over to Lola, and said, "Open your hand."

"Take these two pills before you have a full migraine. Give them about two minutes to work. The dosage is pretty strong."

"Thank you, Pam. You are the best secretary."

Lola smiled at Pam and added, "And good friend as well. But why are you keeping pills with that strong of a dosage in my office?"

"So I couldn't get to them too easily," Pam said.

Lola stared at her questionably.

"When my marriage was on the rocks, my migraines were so bad at the office, as good as those pills worked, I was afraid I would take too many if I kept them in my office. Of course, I haven't needed one in a while now that Ryan and I are doing much better in our marriage."

"Maybe I better keep them in my purse, cause, girl my migraine is just about gone," Lola said, feeling so much better.

Pam sat in front of Lola's desk, smiled at Lola and began talking.

"My mamma told me something a long time ago. I didn't quite understand it all then, but I sure learned later in life. I hope it makes sense to you because Lord knows it helped save my marriage."

Lola smiled at her secretary.

"And what did your mamma tell you that was so important later in life?" Lola asked, migraine gone.

"I mean, you are only what...about twenty-two?"

"Age has nothing to do with being ignorant and stupid, Ms. Lola. Trust me, I was both. That being said, mom told me that sometimes in life you have to be careful who you share your happiness with. I did not listen and almost lost one of the best things that ever happened to me."

"And what was that?" Lola asked, smiling.

"My husband. I made the mistake of telling my best friend, who wasn't really my best friend at all, how wonderful my husband was to me."

"How good he was to me…in and out the bed. I thought it was okay to tell her since she was telling me how wonderful her husband was, and how good he was to her…in and out the bed."

"Turns out she was not married and did not even have a boyfriend. She only wanted to befriend me because she wanted my husband in every way. In and out the bed. She wanted my house."

"My husband. Everything. She even wanted the car I'm driving. Especially since my husband bought me that car for my birthday."

"Long story short, she even made up lies just so I could tell her things about my husband so she would know his likes and dislikes. Truth be told, she wanted my life."

"You said almost. What happened? If it's too personal you don't have to tell me," Lola explained.

"No. It's okay. You see, Ms. Lola, I married a good man. A real man who truly loves me."

"One day he told me that Ina, my so-called best friend, was not my friend at all. When I tried to argue with him about it he then asked me, 'if she truly is your best friend why is she trying so hard to sleep with me?'

"Oh my God," Lola whispered.

"Did he sleep with her?"

"No. Well not exactly."

"What do you mean, not exactly?'

"Ryan, that's my husband's name, told me he went to her apartment to have sex with her. While they were kissing, my face stood between them. Said his love for me hit him like a ton of bricks."

"He explained how shame washed over him and all he wanted to do was get out of there. He told me he stopped kissing Ina, apologized and ran from the apartment and never looked back."

"When she continued to harass him to sleep with her and he wouldn't, she told him she would tell me he tried to rape her. That's when he knew he had to tell me."

"If you don't mind my asking, why would he want to sleep with this Ina girl anyway? Pam, you are gorgeous. Talk about a pretty young thing...girl you are it."

Lowering her eyes in shame, Pam explained, "Thank you, Ms. Lola, but gorgeous and nagging your man to death just because I couldn't have my way don't go together. I got mad at Ryan one day because I couldn't have my way and told him he was not a man and that no other woman wanted him."

"First he looked at me like I was stupid and from another planet, turned and walked out the room. Ina had been eyeing my husband ever since before we got married, but I was so blind and stupid I didn't see it."

"I had a talk with mom about the situation thinking she was going to take my side. Trust me when I tell you, I wised up very quickly after our talk. Mom did not pull any punches."

"Not only did she not take my side, she told me I was a spoiled child that had turned into a spoiled woman. Told me I didn't deserve a man like Ryan and that if I lost him it was my own fault."

"Her next question, Ms. Lola, I will never forget."

"What did she say?" Lola asked when Pam just stared into space.

"Mom asked, 'Why were you telling another woman about your man and the intimacy y'all share in the first place? You handed your man to this girl on a silver platter.'

"I came to my senses very quickly. I realized that more women I cared to count wanted my husband. I apologized to Ryan. Explained to him how mom and dad had spoiled me rotten until they saw what it was doing to me and started damage control. Of course, some things I stubbornly carried into my adult life."

"I had a long talk with my husband. Apologized for the mean words I said. Once Ryan understood my early life better, he began to understand me better as a woman. He apologized to me for kissing another woman and I learned to respect my husband and keep my marriage business between my husband and I and things have been great ever since."

"Is Ryan the man who came to take you to lunch the other day?" Lola asked.

Pam smiled. "Yes."

"And that is the man you told that he was not a man and that no other woman would want him? The man that is a walking advertisement for GQ? The man no woman can look at just once? Including me?"

Pam burst out laughing.

"Yes. That man is my husband. That was three years ago, Ms. Lola. I was very stupid and ignorant. I made the mistake of calling my husband out on his masculinity and almost lost the true love of my life."

"I thank God my mother and father saw their mistake and what it was doing to me. I know my husband is absolutely gorgeous and very handsome. All six feet, two inches of him."

"I'm just so happy his love for me stopped him before he had sex with that crazy woman or any other woman."

Pam looked at Lola and smiled.

"So please, Ms. Lola, be very careful of the happiness you share with others. Especially about the man in your life."

"I can understand why your friend is skeptical and cautious about you dating a man from an online dating sites, but not to the point of carrying on the way she did a few minutes ago."

"Point taken. Thank you, Pam. When you finish your work you can leave. I have a date Friday night. I'm not going shopping, but I think I will get my hair done."

"Good for you, Ms. Lola. You know what they say...let your hair down and enjoy the ride."

"Thank you, Pam. Oh, and Pam?"

"Yes?"

"Where did you put those pills?"

"I am taking them with me, Ms. Lola," Pam smiled, on the verge of outright laughing.

"I haven't needed them in a while, but you might be needing them often between Ms. Anna and your date. If you need some, just let me know."

Pam smiled lovingly, "Ms. Wells, you are the best boss I ever had and we can't have you getting upset and needing these pills too often."

"Oh, rats. What if you are not here and I need them?"

"I left a few in your office. I got your back, Ms. Lola."

"Thanks, Pam."

At the door, Pam turned and smiled. "And, Ms. Lola?"

"Yes?"

"You have truly made my day about the age thing. I am twenty-eight...not twenty-two."

Lola smiled as Pam left her office.

Driving home from the hair salon her phone rang through her Bluetooth in her car. Cautiously, Lola answered.

"Hey, Anna."

"Don't you hey Anna me in that dry tone of voice," Anna lightly scolded.

"You didn't tell me you were leaving early today. I called to apologize for my outburst in your office and Pam said you were gone for the day."

"I had some things I needed to take care of," Lola said dryly.

"Lola, where are you?"

"Why?"

"Lola, girl if I have to sleep on your doorstep until you get home I am coming over. Now cut the attitude with me."

Lola had to laugh. If nothing else, Anna was persistent.

"I will be home in thirty five minutes."

Anna was waiting when she got there. She gave a low whistle when Lola exited her car.

"So that's where you took off too. Girl, I love the hair."

"Thanks," Lola said, unlocking the door and walking to the stairs.

"Let me get comfortable. You know to make yourself at home. I'll be down in a minute."

"Take your time. In the meanwhile, I will be raiding your kitchen for food."

"You won't find much," Lola said from the stairs.

"I haven't grocery shopped yet."

Fifteen minutes later Lola saw Anna take the last bite of a sandwich she thought she had thrown out.

"Anna, I was going to throw out that sandwich as soon as I got to the refrigerator. I bought it last week. It was too old. I hope you don't get sick."

"Tasted alright to me. For a backup I prayed God's blessings over it," Anna said, swallowing the last bite and rinsing it down with a bottle of water.

Sitting Indian style with both legs under her, Anna apologized to her friend.

"I don't mean to be so negative about your date, Lola, but I still have nightmares from Frank trying to kill me."

"And I thank you, Anna, for caring so much, but Hunter and I are not going to the altar to get married. We are going on a date…in a public well-lit place. And what happened in my office? Why did you get so upset? The man sent me flowers, not a timed bomb."

"Lola, how did he know where you work? I am sorry, Lola, but for now I just don't trust him."

"You have a right to your opinion and I thank you for caring so much. You don't have to trust Hunter. Like I have been wasting my breath telling you for the twelfth time that it is only a date in a very public place. Now please, no more talk about my date."

Reaching for her phone, she told Anna, "I'm ordering hot wings and pizza. Are you staying to help me eat all this food?"

"Bite your tongue, Lola," Anna said, relaxing her feet from under her.

"That sandwich only made me hungrier. Do you have wine?"

Lola held up her hand to stop her friend from talking when the lady answered to take her order.

Swiping the phone off Lola laid her head back and took a deep breath and exhaled slowly.

Watching her friend through half closed eyes, she said, "Yes, I have wine. Your favorite. And to answer your question about Hunter knowing where I work…"

Lola almost laughed at her friend's serious facial expression and body language. Anna sat up very straight as if she was about to learn the best kept secret since turning lemons into lemonade.

"When I was about to tell him where I worked he quickly stopped me."

"No, please don't tell me where you work," he said, "and I could tell he was smiling on the other end of the phone."

"Why? I asked him?"

"I already know where you work," he told me.

"I asked him how he knew since I hadn't told him. Trust me. By now, you better believe me, my Spidey senses were tingling. I felt he was toying with me."

"He then gave a little chuckle and said he would tell me Friday night."

If anything, Anna was more furious.

"That is a bunch of crock," she exclaimed as she stood trying very hard to control her temper.

"I'm going to take a quick shower before the food gets here," Lola said, choosing not to comment on her friend's furious outburst.

Hours later after two full stomachs and two empty bottles of wine, "Oooh, I stuffed myself. Those were the best wings and pizza I have eaten in a long while," Anna groaned.

"I hear ya," Lola agreed. "I tried that new restaurant down the street since they had delivery service.

However, you better believe it will be a while before I order there again. Their food is too good and tasty."

"I hope you don't think you are going to sleep on that couch, Anna," Lola said, laughing as she started moving furniture.

"Girl, why are you moving that furniture?" Anna asked, already knowing the answer.

Lola looked at her friend and raised both eyebrows.

"There is only one reason I move the coffee table and you know what that means."

Anna groaned. "Not tonight, Lola. I am too stuffed to move. I'm sleepy."

"It's either WII Sports or dancing to some golden oldies."

Anna already had one leg comfortably resting on the couch.

2

"Aww, come on, Anna. Just a little dancing. We won't do the WII Sports." Lola gave a heavy sigh.

"Now, Anna, you know we can't go to bed this stuffed. That food was so good we did something tonight we have never done."

"What is that?" Anna yawned.

"We ate the entire pizza…a large three topping and all the wings. Plus we finished off two bottles of wine."

Lola sighed again. "Do I need to remind you again that it was a large three toppings pizza…and fifteen wings? Fifteen, Anna."

"One night of splurging won't hurt that figure of yours," Anna said.

"Seems like the more you eat, the better you look. Now I'm not gonna lie, Lola, you are a beautiful black woman and sometimes I do envy you. If I didn't love men so much I swear I would give any man a run for his money to have you. That body of yours is to die for."

Looking down at her body, Anna wailed, "Lola why did you have to be so beautiful? I am the one who needs to lose some pounds. Maybe that is why Frank went knife-crazy on me."

"Girl, please," Lola said, smiling at her friend.

"You are a size ten. Your skin is flawless and you're gorgeous. Frank just loved preying on beautiful, rich young women. And you are beautiful and you make good money, and you have a nice home. Now come on, let's burn some of these calories."

"Okay, girl," Anna agreed.

"Let's burn some of these cals," she sighed, falling back on the couch. A minute later, she was snoring.

"Anna, girl, wake up. That's not fair. You promised."

"What's not fair?" Anna asked, getting more comfortable on the couch.

"We'll talk about it in the morning. Love you girl," she sighed, emitting a loud snore.

Thinking of her date on Friday night, wanting to look her best, Lola decided to play tennis with the WII Sports game even if her friend was knocked out on the couch.

Thirty minutes into the game, beginning to sweat, she wanted to try her hand at boxing next.

Having never used boxing before, ten minutes into boxing, Lola realized she loved it. Especially when she pictured Frank as the punching bag.

Feeling proud of herself after fifteen more minutes of boxing she called it quits finishing with a few deep breaths and stretch exercises.

Lola stared at the coffee table, "You will be just fine where you are until morning."

Tapping Anna on the shoulder she told her to wake up it was time for bed.

The snoring continued.

"Anna, come on, wake up. It is time for bed. Your room is right down the hall."

"Okay," she said, turning over on the couch. "Good night, Lola. You are my best friend and I love you, girl." The snoring continued.

Covering her with the thick throw, Lola told her good night.

"I will never feed you that much food again. Especially, if we top it off with your favorite wine. Love you right back," Lola said as she walked up the stairs.

"I must love you to let you sleep on my three thousand dollar white couch I ordered from Italy," Lola mused. "At least I feel about thirty pounds lighter."

Friday…The Date

"I should not be this excited over just one date," Lola whispered to herself.

Staring at herself in the mirror there was sadness in her eyes. Although Anna had apologized for her distrust of Hunter, she missed her from helping her get dressed.

"Anna, girl you are my best friend. You could have at least showed up and gave me a little support."

Remembering Pam's words of caution, she whispered, "Maybe I am to walk this path alone. Lord please protect me if Hunter is not the man for me. Guard my heart. Give me the strength to walk away if I have to. Amen"

Looking the best she could look, with purse in hand she softly closed the door and walked to her garage.

At the entrance of the restaurant, a man dressed in a tux was waiting for her.

"Ms. Wells? Lola Wells?"

"Yes. I'm Ms. Wells."

"If you will come with me, Ms. Wells."

"Thank you."

Goodness, do I have a stain on my dress or something, she pondered. All eyes appear to be on me.

Hunter stared at the woman walking towards him dumb struck. If I could, I would propose to her tonight. *Finally, I have found my wife,* he thought.

There is a God and after years of searching, my prayer has been answered.

A few steps away from their table, he stood and pulled out her chair. Her nervous smile rocked his world.

"Ms. Wells, how are you?"

Before she answered Hunter, she turned and thanked the waiter for escorting her to the table.

Lola sat down with Hunter's assistance and waited until he was seated before she answered his question.

"I'm well. How are you?"

"I am fine."

My God, but yes you are fine, she thought. He was not overly dressed, but the suit he had on was made for his body alone.

The black leisure jacket, gray turtleneck pullover, and charcoal slacks only made him look more distinguished. The watch on his wrist and silver chain around his neck that ended with a locket-like medallion that rested on his chest were priceless.

Yes, Mr. Hunter you are so fine. Lola hastily reigned her thoughts back in.

Hoping he could not read her thoughts, she quickly asked, "Were you waiting long? I hope I'm not too late?"

For the first time in forty one years he didn't know what to do with his hands.

Come on Hunter, he chided himself, *she is only a woman. Fool, get yourself together.*

She is not just a woman, his mind argued, *this is my wife. The mother of my children. The woman I want to grow old with.*

"No. You are not late. I was a few minutes early. Is it okay that I ordered the wine for us? Of course, if you don't like it, you can order what you prefer."

After the wine was poured and the waiter left, she tasted it.

"Umm. This is really good."

She is easy to please, he thought.

"This place is really lovely, but you didn't have to bring me here. I don't need to be impressed with this kind of wining and dining."

Taking a sip of wine, he slowly placed the glass on the table, eyes never leaving hers. "What do you need...to be impressed, Lola?"

Say my name. Say...my...name, she shouted in her mind. *I am so glad I prayed before I left the house. This man is no amateur when it comes to dining women. And how am I supposed to answer that question?*

"Well, I mean, I don't need all this," she said, looking around at all the grandeur. "After all it's just a date. I would like to get to know you better. The man. Not so much the food or this lovely restaurant."

"There is always a first date, Lola. I didn't bring you here to impress you. I chose this restaurant because I love coming here and was hoping you would as well. I can eat at a Burger King, McDonald's or any other place I choose. I would be the same man. The eating place doesn't change who I am as a man."

Hunter got her attention with his eyes and held them in his stare.

"I would be less than a man if I had taken you to Burger King tonight. Maybe later, when we get to know each other better, we can grab a burger, fries and go to the park, but not tonight. You are absolutely worth being here tonight. It appeared as if all eyes turned your way when you walked in the door. And, Lola?"

Talk about taking someone's breath away. With what little breath she had left, she whispered, "Yes?"

"Zooming. Skyping. Did not do you justice. You are absolutely gorgeous and that dress looks lovely on you. Burger King, McDonald's, or even Olive Garden would not have done you or that dress justice this evening."

"Thank you. You look very handsome yourself."

"Thank you, Lola."

The atmosphere was changing at the table and they both could feel it. Lola felt things were moving too fast. *Oh, Lord. How do I stop this feeling? I'm about ready to jump as high as he wants me to.*

Okay Lola, just keep your mouth shut and listen to what he is or is not saying, she thought, taking a sip of wine.

"What if I want there to be a second date?" He asked.

God. I am half way in bed with this man, she prayed. *Please help.*

"Can we at least get through the first date? We might not want there to be a second date," Lola said, knowing she was lying through her teeth.

"Would you like to order or do you need more time?" Hunter asked, needing to take it slow.

If I had my way we would get married tomorrow.

"I'm ready to order, but I don't see any prices."

"Don't worry about the prices. Order what you want." Hunter stared into her eyes and got her attention. "And, Lola?"

"Yes?"

"This dinner comes with no strings attached. I just want to enjoy a nice evening at dinner with the most beautiful woman I have ever seen."

"Wow! Hunter. You definitely know how to make a girl feel special. Thank you. I'm ready to order."

Fort Knox, God. Heart needs to be guarded with a thirty foot steel door, she prayed. *I didn't know men could be this nice and charming.*

Hunter could feel her nervousness across the table. Hoping to ease her nervousness, he commented on the restaurant and how he knew the place.

"This restaurant is actually rather old," he explained. "Nick, a colleague of mine, and some friends put me on to this place."

"The food is really good and the atmosphere is very pleasant. People tend to mind their own business. After a hard day's work it's really a great place to come eat as you wind down."

"Do you come here often? I remember you told me you lived in Chicago."

"I do live in Chicago, but when I need to complete an assignment for work in Atlanta, this is my favorite restaurant."

Wondering if he should say his next words, he decided to make his intentions clear. *I didn't get where I am today by cowering down,* he thought.

"I'm hoping to come more often since talking to you on the phone and having dinner with you tonight."

Hunter smiled and said humorously, "I loved our talks on the phone, skyping, and zooming. Now that we meet face to face, I love this even better."

Is that my heart beating out of my chest or drums deciding to use my heart for hire, Lola thought.

The Online Date

Saved by the food from having to answer right away she tried pulling herself together.

Okay, I am acting very childish, just go with the flow. So far he is being a gentleman. Looking at the food that was placed in front of her,

"I'm surprised our food came back so quickly. This place is full. There is not an empty table, and yet, our meal came back promptly," Lola mentioned when about six minutes after ordering, the food was being served.

It did not get past him that she did not respond to his statement.

"They are prepared for this. One of the reasons there are no prices on the menu," he explained instead.

Taking a bite of sliced roast and potatoes, Lola was very impressed.

"Umm," she moaned, "this is very good. This roast melts in my mouth. Thank you again for dinner."

"You are very welcome, Lola. I was hoping you would like it." Laying down her fork, she stared at Hunter.

Alright, Mr. Hunter, Lola was thinking. *That is about the fifth time you have said my name. Are you too good to be true? Are you a pervert who gets off on names? Maybe Anna was right. Should I leave before he breaks through Fort Knox and steals my heart? I need some answers.*

"Why do you continue to say my name in almost every sentence?" She blurted out.

"Do I frighten you when I say your name, Lola?" This time he whispered her name.

"A little. I mean I don't know you."

"Would you rather I not call your name as much?"

"Yes. Please. I don't mean to be rude, but I'd rather you didn't."

"It won't happen again." He could almost see the change in her. A defensive wall she had barricaded against me. I intend to tear it down.

"I am sorry for making you uncomfortable. In my defense, I love your name. I love saying it."

This is the perfect time to ask my question…before I take another bite of food so good it melts in my mouth, she thought.

"You had flowers delivered to my office and truly they are lovely. I enjoyed getting them. Remember you were going to explain how you knew where I worked."

Patience, Hunter, he thought.

If she can't relax and learn to trust me, she can't fall in love with me.

Laying down his fork as well, he told her as much as he could without telling her exactly what he did.

"I work for a private firm. I also work part-time as an Investigative Consultant for the government. I can get anyone's address. Of course knowing everyone's address is of no importance to me. Actually, it's not as hard as people may think."

Taking a sip of his wine, he said, "Now you, Ms. Wells. I like you. I wanted to celebrate our almost six weeks of talking. Getting to know each other better. So I sent you five roses. One for each week, and I needed your work address to do that. A few clicks on the computer and there was your address and the building where you work."

"I don't mean to be so suspicious, but a woman has to be careful."

"Say no more. I really do understand. I hate online dating, but my sister gave me a dare. She won. That is how I ended up on that website."

"If you don't mind me asking, what was the dare?"

"I told her I could get a date that was not an online date by a certain time. I lost and here we are."

He held out his hands as if in defeat before continuing with his meal.

Mm, hmm, Lola thought. *You must not have tried too hard. There is not a woman on earth who would not have gone out with you. Well maybe a few happily married ladies. There is something you are not telling me, Mr. Hunter Nichols.*

Lola picked up her fork and finished her scrumptious meal.

"Would you like a cup of coffee?" Hunter asked when they finished their meal. "More wine?"

"No thank you," Lola said, tapping at the corners of her mouth with her napkin.

"I really enjoyed dinner, Hunter." *I enjoyed you as well, but that will not come through my lips tonight,* Lola thought.

"Thank you. Trust me, the pleasure was all mine," Hunter said.

Not really wanting the night to end, Lola was hoping he would ask to prolong the date, but she didn't know him well enough to actually go someplace if he did ask her.

"The River-walk is lit up at night if you would like to go. It's still kind of early and lots of people are still out walking enjoying the moonlight. It is only two minutes from here."

Before she changed her mind and said she would love to go, Lola quickly said, "Maybe another time. I really do have to leave."

Lola reached across the table to shake Hunter's hand so she could leave, go home and think about what could have been with this fine man. Cause Lord, I know this man is not going to call me back for date number two.

"Thank you, Hunter, for such a lovely dinner. I thoroughly enjoyed it."

Lola scanned the room. The place was beautiful. People were minding their own business. At least no one was staring at her like they did when she first walked in. She spread out her hands to encase everything before laying her hands close to his.

"I enjoyed everything about this evening."

He closed her hands inside his and shock waves ran through her entire body. Hunter gently rubbed her palms, eyes never leaving hers.

"I would really like to see you again. A few Skype, zooms and even this dinner is not enough to truly get to know you. Seeing you in person only makes me want to get to know you even better."

Is it possible for someone to make love to your hands? She thought, frighteningly, as she tried to ease them away. *Lord, this man is dangerous.*

Reading her mind correctly, he put her at ease. "And, yes, Ms. Wells. Not to worry. We will meet in a public place." He smiled. "As a matter of fact, this time you choose the place."

"Will you be in town long? I don't want to get you in trouble with your job."

You wonderful woman, he thought. *She is thoughtful and considerate as well.*

"I am in town for as long as you need me to be. Name the place and I will be there."

Is it too early to be weak in the knees? Lola asked herself.

"Can I think on it tonight and text you the place tomorrow?"

"Yes. That will be okay as long as you text me."

Getting up from his chair Hunter came and stood by her chair and reached for her hand.

"Come on."

"What are you doing?" Lola asked, a little skeptical.

"Helping you from your seat so I can walk you to your car. It is dark outside and I don't want you walking alone."

Lord, where is that steel door? My heart needs a little help. This man knows all the right things to say.

"Can I ask you a question and you not get mad at me?" Hunter asked.

"I don't know. I need to hear the question first."

"Do you have a security system where you live?"

"I am not mad at the question, Hunter. I just don't understand the need for the question."

"Sometimes in my line of work I work with the police to help find unsavory people. I like you, Ms. Wells and people I like, I need to know they are safe."

"Fair enough. Yes, I have home security. Top of the line."

"That's my girl," Hunter whispered, but she heard.

Lord, I don't mind being this man's girl forever, she thought. *So long as he is as real as he appears, Lord. Cause' Lord you know Cra' cra' come in all sizes. Handsome and tall.*

Hunter wanted to kiss Lola so bad, but knew it was too soon. *Calm down, man and wait. Like mom always told me… 'Good things come to those that wait.'*

"Good night, Ms. Wells."

"Good night, Hunter." Lola paused before her next words. "And, Hunter?"

"Yes?"

"You can call me Lola. It's only fair since I call you Hunter."

He smiled and gently touched her face. "You mentioned earlier that I did not have to do all this…" He waved his hand to encompass the restaurant.

"You deserved all this and more. Trust me, you are worth it…and more. Dining with you tonight…being the envy of every man here, was totally my pleasure. And that red dress should be illegal. All eyes were on you tonight. Drive safely, Lola. Remember to text me our meeting place."

"Okay," she breathed softly.

Safely in her car, he closed her door and watched until the tail lights were out of view. Dialing a number on his phone, when someone picked up, Hunter spoke.

"Yeah, man. She is on the way home, but something is off. I can feel it in my bones," Hunter said, scanning the area.

"Whatever you do, don't let her out of your sight."

Hunter listened to the comments from the other end. "Look man. I know the drill. Don't tell me not to get involved. I'm already involved. Just make sure she gets home safely. Now that is an order and what you get paid to do."

"You low down, dirty dog," Anna whispered.

"Lola, I told you that man was not to be trusted." Anna rushed to her car across the parking lot hoping to meet Lola when she got home. Meanwhile, across the street a sinister voice came from the bushes.

"You won't be able to protect her forever Mr. whatever your name is. Lola is mine and I mean to have her," the voice whispered vehemently from the shadows.

3

"Hello?"

"Lola?"

"Anna, girl is this you? I am picking up some static."

"Yeah, it's me. Lola, I need you at my house now!"

Talk about a dinner damper, Lola thought.

All I want to do is go home and think about how good dinner was and the man that made it all possible. Not Anna threatening to ruin it all.

"Anna what is wrong? Did you forget I had dinner tonight? A date you were supposed to…"

"Lola, I *was* at dinner tonight."

"Oh, I get it," Lola said, smiling to herself. "You want me to come over and we talk about our dates. Okay. You probably want to talk about you and Sam getting closer. I hope your dinner was as nice as mine. I'll see you in a bit."

"Hey boss."

"Yeah. What is it, Nick?"

"She is not going home."

"What do you mean she is not going home?"

"She stopped at a gas station…"

"Well, maybe she is stopping to get gas," Hunter said, heart rate accelerating.

"She did not get out of the car. She kinda made a U-turn at the station and now she is going in the direction she came."

"Can you still see her?"

"Yeah."

"Please. Just try not to lose her. And, Nick?"

"Yeah, boss?"

"If you do lose her. Call me yesterday."

"Damn, boss," Nick said humorously, "you really care about this one don't you?"

"Get off the phone so you can concentrate on not losing Ms. Wells, Nick."

Minutes later Lola was ringing Anna's doorbell. On the first ring Anna opened the door and pulled Lola in, closed the door and double locked it.

"Wow!" Lola said happily. "This must have been some date. I knew you and Sam were getting serious. I was right ha," Lola said, raising her eyebrows.

"Here, drink this. You are going to need it," Anna said, handing her a hot steaming cup of chamomile tea she had prepared.

Taking a sip, Lola held her head back in total enjoyment.

"Mm. This tea is really good," she said, taking another sip.

Placing the cup on the cup holder, she said, "Now tell me about this man who is stealing your heart? My date actually turned out better than I expected. But, first, I want to hear about this man that is so great. I know it is Sam. Girl, I had to turn around at this gas station and…"

"Lola, please. Just stop. Please," Anna wailed.

Oh, Lord, Anna thought. *How am I gonna tell her that Hunter is no good?*

Taking a deep breath, Anna decided to just blurt everything out.

"I did not go on a date with Sam tonight. Sam and I are getting serious, but…"

"Well what is the problem? If you are not talking about your date, what are you talking about?"

"Lola, I went to the restaurant that you went to tonight."

"Why? You told me you were not going so I just prayed and trusted my own instincts." Lola smiled. "I truly enjoyed the dinner and Hunter was a perfect…"

"Lola, can I get a word in edgewise?"

"Okay, Anna. What are you trying to tell me?"

"Lola. Honey I am so sorry to tell you this, but Hunter is no good, and…"

"Wait a minute," Lola almost shouted as she stood and stared at Anna.

"Wait just a minute. You mean to tell me you sneaked behind my back. Went to the restaurant. Spied on us and did not tell me! You told me you were not coming."

"What I said was in anger, Lola. I always meant to come to the restaurant. Actually, I am glad that I did. I have to tell you what I heard Hunter say after you left. He called someone immediately after you left. He said something was off and he wanted someone to follow you. Please listen to me, Lola. Let him go. Don't ever talk to him again. Don't end up like me."

Lola picked up her purse from the couch and turned to leave.

"Where are you going?"

"I am going home. I could have been at home safe inside. Instead, I turn around and come here thinking you had good news to tell me about you and Sam. Ever since I told you about Hunter you have not given us a chance. Even though I told you we were meeting in a public place. You are the one who got me going back out in the dark to go home…alone. Cause I refuse to stay the night with you."

"I thought maybe you would want to stay the night here...with me after what I told you. Please, Lola. You know I love you. Stay here tonight. I am sorry."

"Good night, Anna," Lola said, walking to the door.

"Call me and let me know when you get home," Anna shouted to Lola, but she had closed the door behind her.

"Wait, boss. Hold on. I see her. She is coming out now. You don't have to come."

"Find out who lives there and how often she goes to that address," Hunter instructed.

"Boss, are you sure you want to go down this road? Me and the boys were talking and we have never seen you taken with a woman like this before."

"Nick, just make sure she gets home safe."

Hunter swiped his card to the hotel door and went and laid on the couch. Sighing deeply, he thought about what Nick said.

When his firm got the call about a woman needing protection, they had been talking on the phone for three weeks before he knew that Lola and the woman needing protection were one and the same person.

When they zoomed each other on their computers, he hid his shock very well. Her face and the picture sent to him were the same.

By then he was already falling for her. When he saw her at the restaurant earlier tonight, he knew his search for a wife was over.

"How do I tell someone you are supposedly protecting that you love them? She is just going to tell me that I lied to her and refuse to see me again."

His cell phone rang so loud, he jumped before answering.

"Yeah?"

"She is home and safely inside, boss."

"Thank you, Nick. Man you are the best. Go home to your family before that lovely wife of yours puts you out and blame me for it."

"Missy understands, especially since we used to be partners. You sure you're okay, boss?"

"Yeah, Nick. I'm good. Tell Missy hello."

Snuggling under the warm covers, Lola knew exactly where she wanted their next date to take place.

"Good night, Hunter," she whispered, feeling all warm inside. "I hope you are thinking of me, cause' I can't get you out of my mind."

Her doorbell woke her the next morning.

"Who is ringing my doorbell at this hour?" Lola said walking slowly down the stairs.

"I'm coming," she shouted at the bell's continued ringing.

Peeping through the peephole, she slowly opened the door and walked back into the room to turn off the alarm.

"Oh, so no good morning? No hello. No, I am still in the land of the living," Anna rattled on following Lola to the kitchen.

"Lola, have you nothing to say? I waited on a call last night. A text or something."

Lola looked at her best friend, but did not smile. "Anna, why are you here?"

"Why am I…?" Anna started the sentence but could not finish it as tears welled in her eyes.

"I am here because I care."

"As you can see I am fine. You don't have to stay…" Lola stopped when she saw the crushed look on Anna's face.

Anna's face crumbled as the tears fell. With purse in hand she turned to rush out the door feeling more hurt than ever.

Lola stopped her before she opened the door.

"Anna, please I am sorry. I was being a bitch and I am sorry."

Lola walked to the door and held Anna as she sobbed, realizing how badly she had hurt her friend.

"Come on. I'll make breakfast and coffee."

Anna raised her head from Lola's shoulder. "I don't want to be here if you don't want me here."

"I want you here. You are my best friend. I just need for you to not hound me every ten minutes about Hunter. I promise you I am being very careful. Our next date is going to be at the Zoo. And you know how crowded our Zoo can be during our peak season."

The Online Date

Sipping her coffee, Anna asked, "So you decided on having another date?"

Anna held both hands up in defense.

"Don't bite my head off, Lola. I'm just making small talk. That's all. I mean, you know how nice Frank was at the beginning of our dates. I thought the man could do no wrong."

"But Anna, you know I never lied to you about disliking Frank. Something was off about him from the start. I tried to give him the benefit of the doubt because you did care so much for him."

"But Frank didn't give me too much of a choice to like him. I always got a bad vibe around Frank. I mean, did you ever notice the way he just stared at me all the time? Like he would ravish me if he could. There was always something about his eyes."

"Well, I still think you maybe wanted Frank just a little bit for yourself and you saw what you wanted to see. I mean, the man was fine," Anna said in defense of Frank.

"He wasn't that fine. He looked okay. Well, maybe to you he was fine. I can't argue with that. And that is beside the point. You know I would never flirt with my best friend's guy. I don't care if he was God's gift to every woman, I never would have crossed that line with you and your boyfriend, and you know it."

"Yeah, I know you are right. I did not want to admit it to myself. I was actually glad that a man like Frank would skip over you and date me."

Staring at her friend, Lola couldn't believe what she was hearing. "Skip over me!" Lola exclaimed.

"Anna, Frank was not all that and a bag of chips. Frank was a scary looking man at best. We all saw it. Even Sam said something to me about him."

"He caught him looking at me a couple of times himself. The man became aroused just staring at me. When he saw Sam and me staring below his waist, he then kissed you in front of us to throw us off."

"Well, it was still nice to have a man of that caliber to skip you and choose me," Anna said, refusing to admit that Frank, on most occasions, acted as if he wanted Lola instead of her. Lola refused to answer Anna, afraid of what she might say.

Changing the subject, Anna continued, "And another thing. Sam never said anything to me about liking me back then."

"Sam liked you before you met Frank. He didn't want to hurt you because he knew how you felt about Frank, so he said nothing."

Lola eyed Anna above her coffee cup and smiled mischievously before saying, "Now if you truly want to see a man that truly has it all…and not just looks, is my secretary's husband."

Anna eyed Lola suspiciously. "Ooh, so you are lusting after married men now ha."

"Girl no. I truly admire Pam's husband. He truly loves his wife and appears to be dedicated to her. Lusting after married men is a total waste of time."

The only man that is worth my while lusting after is Hunter, Lola thought, getting up from the table before Anna noticed her change of color to her face.

Hoping to cheer Anna up after their spat last night, she said, "While I take care of the dishes, why don't you relax in the living room. I am taking you shopping when I'm done."

With tears filling her eyes, Anna stared at Lola in awe.

"Really? You would do that for me? After I was so mean to you about your friend."

"Of course, I will do that for you." Lola sat down at the table and held Anna's hands in hers.

"We have always done for each other. We did not always have these great jobs that pay so well. But, what we had we always shared. Frank did a number on you. And by the grace of God you are still with us today."

"I know you love me and don't want to see me get hurt. Hunter and I are trying to get to know each other better. All I ask of you is to give me a little credit for being careful. We have been talking going on two months and he has not set foot in my home. We have not kissed. Not one time."

"Okay," Anna muffled on Lola's shoulder.

"Now that that's out the way, I will finish the dishes. We will leave in fifteen minutes."

"First, we will start with a mani-pedi. Then we are going to Macy's."

"What is at Macy's?" Anna asked.

"I believe the last time we were there someone was eyeing a certain purse."

"Oh, Lola!" Anna exclaimed.

"I can't let you buy that purse. The reason I didn't get it was because it would have set me back more than one of my paychecks…and my check is no peanuts. Lola, please don't spend that much money on a stupid purse."

"Are you ready?" Lola asked when she finished the dishes.

"Yes."

They walked out the house laughing at a joke Anna was sharing with her. Seat belts safely on, Lola backed from the garage, looked at Anna and said, "I love you girl."

"Love you back," Anna said, happily as they drove down the road.

"How's it going with Sam?"

Before Anna could comment either way, she exclaimed loudly, "Oh No!"

Pulling into a gas station Lola said, "I sure am glad we had not gotten on the expressway. Girl, what is wrong? Why are you tossing and turning? What are you looking for?"

Leaning her head back on the headrest, she wailed, "Lola I am so sorry but I think I left my purse at your house."

"That's okay isn't it? I mean I am paying for everything today. Can't you get it when we come back?"

Instead of answering Lola, Anna burst out crying.

Lola had noticed Anna had been crying a lot lately. Anything would set her off. Good news. Bad news. Sometimes no news. Lately if it rained, she would softly begin to weep.

Without saying anything, Lola turned around at the gas station and headed for home.

After she parked, Lola turned to her friend, held her hand gently and asked, "Anna, are you pregnant?"

"I think so." Anna's lips began to tremble as the tears began to fall again.

"How many months?"

"Maybe three."

"Have you told Sam?"

"No."

"Why not, Anna?"

"Because I told him I could not have any children and that it was safe and he didn't need to take precautions."

"Oh, Anna," Lola said and pulled her into her arms.

"Lola, what am I going to do? Sam said he hated children. Said they were a nuisance. I didn't know I loved him so much until I got pregnant with his baby and the intimacy we shared to get this child."

Lola held Anna away from her.

"Do you want this baby? I mean are you going to keep it if you have to choose between Sam and the baby?"

"I don't even have to think twice. Hands down, the baby comes first. Yes. I am keeping the baby."

"That's my girl. He or she already has a god-mother. I will always be there for you…and my little god-baby. Now let's go see where you left your purse and let's go celebrate the good news."

At the door they looked at each other and burst out laughing. "We're having a baby!" Lola squealed in excitement.

"Yeah, Nick. What is it?"

"Whoever this guy is, he is not giving up. Someone was hanging around the back of her home pretending to be some kind of cable guy. Uniform and all. He didn't look suspicious at all. Anyone walking by would think he was checking on her cable, but I knew what to look for."

"I was about to get from my car and confront him, but the ladies came back. If I didn't know he was up to no good before they came, I knew it then. When he saw them pull up he slowly walked from the back of the house very nonchalantly and got into… would you believe he actually was driving a cable truck. We are dealing with a professional boss."

"Thanks, Nick. I didn't want to do things differently, but now I might not have another choice."

"Hunter, man I hope you are not thinking of telling her who you are and that you were paid to protect her." There was a deafening pause.

"Hunter, man you cannot do that. At least not yet."

"If I don't tell her now, she is going to hate me when she finds out. Lola is not the kind of woman who takes lying lightly."

"So it's Lola now. When did it stop being Ms. Wells?"

"It was Lola before I got the assignment."

"Come again," Nick said, wondering if he heard right.

Heaving a long sigh, Hunter said, "Can you come over. I don't want to say more over the phone?"

"Be there in five."

Five minutes later his doorbell rang.

"Did you transport or something?" Hunter asked, opening the door.

"I was heading your way before I made the call," Nick said, walking into the room.

"Now what is this about Ms. Wells? Are you telling me you knew her before the assignment"?

"Yes! That is exactly what I'm saying."

Hunter sat across from Nick resting his hands between his thighs.

"Let me start from the beginning. I met Lola on a dating site."

"You what? A dating site?"

"You heard me right. A dating site. My sister gave me a dare and I accepted. I even let Stacy set up my profile knowing I was not going to check anybody out anyway."

"The next day my sweet, lovable, nosy, getting into my business little sister told me I had over one-hundred hits. I got curious and decided to see for myself who these women were who were supposed to be compatible with me."

"Out of over one-hundred women there was only one that caused my heart to flutter just by reading her profile. I reached out to her first by text. Two weeks later, by phone, then Skype, and zoom."

"Man, we hit it off from the first text. At first she was very cautious. When I heard her voice, something came over me. Took me weeks before she agreed to go out with me."

"Of course, you know about Friday's dinner. Trust me. She is so much more beautiful in person. When she walked into the restaurant, it appeared as if all eyes were on her. Nick, I want this woman to have all my children. I want to grow old with her."

"It's not just her beauty on the outside, it's how she makes me feel as a man. She fits in my life. She is the only woman I trust to tell my secrets."

"And you, my friend, are the only person that works for me that I am sharing this info with. Stacy, my sister who set up the account doesn't know. Mom and dad don't know."

Staring at Nick, Hunter said, "Man I think…no, I know I am in love with this woman. I not only have to find out who is targeting Lola, I also need to find out why he is targeting her."

"I am torn because we knew each other before I got this assignment. I don't want to lose her, man. I know one of us is probably going to get hurt. Of course I want it to be me. I couldn't stand her being hurt and I was not able to comfort her."

Nick leaned back on the couch and scratched his bald head.

"Dang man. You got it bad. I have seen you with women before, but never like this. But, man I don't think you should tell her yet. If one of those secrets you are so willing to tell her is this assignment, please hold off. You might do more harm than good."

"Did you ever find out who paid you all that money to protect her?"

"No. And trust me, I was not going to take this case because we don't operate like that."

"Yeah. That did surprise me when you took the case without knowing who we are working for."

"Going through the contents of the package for a number to call and explain why we would not be able to take the case, I could not find one. What I did find caused my knees to weaken. I am glad the couch was right behind me or the floor would have caught me."

"What did you find in the papers?"

"A picture of Lola. Five-hundred thousand dollars…in cash, and a note that read, 'When I know that Lola is safe, then and only then will I tell you who I am. The money is good. I just don't need questions arising about that much money being deposited at a bank."

"Did you say five-hundred thousand…?"

"Yes! Of course, I am not touching that kind of money. I need more information."

Hunter walked agitatedly back and forth wearing out the carpet.

"I mean who pays that kind of money to protect someone? Yet he was smart enough to send the letter days before the package arrived."

4

"The only person I can think of is maybe a long lost father who doesn't want to be known," Nick said.

"Her father *is* known. He and his wife, Lola's mom, live in New York. Either way, that is still a lot of money. And I hate all this secrecy. By the time I was asked to take on this assignment, Lola and I were already talking to each other. She had my heart with her first words. Her voice called me and I answered."

"Nick, we are walking into this one blind and I need you and the team to be aware of things that are not there. My heart is deeply involved. Please take nothing for granted. This person is smart. I think he or she knows who I am."

"When are you two going out again?"

"I am waiting for her to text me our next location to meet."

"She probably will pick a public place since she doesn't know you well as of yet."

"She probably will, but I don't mind that. I am glad she is cautious. Hopefully, her being cautious will help save her life."

"When do I get to meet this…?"

Nick's sentence was cut short when Hunter's phone beeped. He went into the other room and read the text.

Walking back into the room he did his best to hide the broad grin on his face but failed.

Not bothering to ask who texted him, he asked instead, "Where is the next meeting taking place?"

"The Zoo. And it is not a meeting, it's a date."

"Boss, please be careful. I don't know what she did to you, but you have fallen hard. I don't want to see you get hurt. Don't let love cloud your judgment of women. She could have a hidden agenda as well. Don't tell her just yet about the assignment. You know you love her, now take this time to get to know her better."

"I need a favor."

"You want me to patrol the zoo. Scope out anything out of the ordinary."

"I know its short notice, but we meet tomorrow evening at three o'clock."

"I will be there. Just be careful. Remember all women are not what they appear. Beauty can hide flaws."

Parking inconspicuously where he was certain of no cameras, he got out of the truck and started walking. "Everything is going as planned," the man said in a menacing voice.

"I will have you yet Ms. Wells. You are mine. You have always been mine."

Opening the door to his old run down house, he threw his hat to the side and stared at all the photos of Lola and started salivating.

"Oh, Lola, you are so beautiful," he said, walking up to one of the pictures and started kissing on it savagely. Turning around to lean against the pictures on the wall, in a rage he tore the picture in his hand to shreds.

"However, my dear Lola, kissing pictures is not enough anymore. I need your body here with me now and that detective or whatever he calls himself will never have you. Yeah. I saw him out with you Friday night."

Walking to the kitchen, he got a knife from the drawer and walked quickly to the room of pictures. Pulling out the desk drawer he took a picture and held it in his hand.

"You Mr. Detective is a very handsome man. My friend Joe would have loved you…that is before I iced him. Of course, I am going to mess up your handsome face."

Laying the picture on the desk he proceeded to stab at the picture until there was nothing left but mutilated pieces of paper.

"Lola is mine. You hear me. Lola is mine, detective and you will not have her."

Walking back to the wall filled with Lola's pictures, he said, crazily with glazed over eyes, "What is your next move my dear? If I can't get past that stupid alarm system you had installed at your beautiful home, I will find another way to get to you. Then I can make you my wife. But I promise I won't hurt you dear."

As crazy thoughts ran rampant in his mind, he turned, stared at the mutilated picture of the detective and whispered, "But first I need to get rid of that detective.

The thought of him ever kissing you makes me so mad I could strangle him with my bare hands."

Walking back to the shredded picture of Hunter, he began stabbing at it again.

The Zoo

Hunter was already at the zoo when Lola arrived. He wanted to watch her as she walked to their meeting place. His heart started doing a double beat.

Oh, God help me because I love her, Hunter prayed silently. *Please don't let her hate me when I have to tell her the truth.*

He noticed she dressed simple with a pair of jeans, a purple blouse and a pair of gym shoes. Her hair was pulled back in a ponytail and held together with a purple and white scarf with purple earrings dangling from her ears.

When she spotted him she gave a quick wave and her smile lit the sky. It reached her beautiful eyes. She was glad to see him.

I should not be this happy to see this man, she thought. "Hunter, how are you?" She said, still smiling.

"I am well. How are you?" He asked, trying hard to hide his true feelings.

Five weeks going on six was way too early to feel what I'm feeling, he told himself.

Holding her hand out to greet him, he grasped it and pulled her slightly to him and kissed her on the cheek. Somewhere between the hellos and the kiss on the cheek, his cologne and her perfume made their way to each other's nostrils.

The stirring of the wind didn't help at all.

Not able to help himself, he pulled her back to him and whispered in her ear.

"I am trying so hard to be a gentleman, Ms. Lola May Wells," he said smiling.

"Whenever, we go on dates please, don't ever wear that perfume again. That scent smells so good it is making me want to do things to your body I should not be thinking, especially this soon."

She burst out laughing at the use of her full name. Hunter waited for her to share her joy.

"Excused me, Hunter for laughing, but you said my full name like my momma used to say when I got into trouble."

Lola wiped the tears from her eyes and stared at Hunter.

Eyes glistening from her tears with little brown flecks shining through, and her smile with lips glowing from the gloss she wore, Hunter was okay in his world. He gently eased her into his arms and held her as their hearts beat to the same rhythm.

"I will stop wearing my perfume if you promise not to wear the cologne you are wearing."

Holding him a little tighter, she whispered, "Mr. Hunter Nichols."

Hunter knew he was in so much trouble when her pliable body held him closer. He eased her from him, took a deep breath, stared her in the eyes and said, "I promise I won't wear it on our next outing."

He tapped her nose and smiled, "My full name, ha?"

"I thought I'd try it out for good measure since my name sounded so wonderful on your lips."

"It did, ha?"

Blushing, Lola thought she had gone too far.

"Hunter David Nichols," Hunter said, easing the tension.

Lola looked at him with a question in her lovely eyes. "Well, my dear, Lola. If you are going to say my full name, let's get it right." He raised his eyebrows twice.

Their laughter mingled together as he reached for her hand and continued their walk.

"Thank you," she whispered. Her breath had long left her.

"For what?" He asked.

"For making me laugh." Instinctively, he pulled her to his side.

Enough children and parents were there for them to act decent and civil, Hunter thought, thankfully as they talked and pointed at the different animals they passed.

They were having so much fun talking and laughing, he did not see the man who walked right past them and stopped a few feet away and just stared at them.

About an hour later Hunter was leading her to his car.

Her smile quickly faded.

"Why are we leaving the zoo?" Lola asked, slowing her steps.

You might wear cologne that smells so good I can sleep with you all night long and the next day as well. Maybe even the day after that, but I am not leaving this zoo away from people with you, she thought.

He eased her hand in his but did not force her any farther and said, "We are not leaving the zoo. I want to show you something. Look around. People are all around. If I try something stupid, scream to the top of your lungs. Start kicking me if that will help."

Lola looked down in shame because he realized what she had been thinking.

"Lola?"

"Yes?"

"Look at me, ba…" Cutting off the word baby in time Hunter was at a loss for words. This woman had him tied in knots.

"Don't ever be ashamed of being cautious. When you texted we were going to the zoo I packed, well the deli packed us a lunch. I was just walking to the car. Would you like to wait here? I will just run to the car."

"No. I will go with you," she said, reaching for his hand. Hunter felt on top of the world because she trusted him.

On the back seat of his car there was a beautiful picnic basket. Hunter got the basket, locked the door, and eased her hand back into his as they walked towards a building down from the animals.

"In case you're wondering, this is the picnic area. Hopefully, there are some tables. My knees do not want the challenge of sitting on the grass today."

"Did you hurt your knees?"

"Yeah, but it was a long time ago."

"I'm sorry about your knees. Do they hurt very badly?"

"Not a lot. Sometimes I can tell when it is going to rain or snow before it does. But enough about me."

Spotting the last bench table, Hunter looked at her, raised his eyebrows, held her hand tighter and ran to the table.

Lola was still laughing when they sat down. She whispered to Hunter, "Did you see that couple racing to this table as well."

"I did, but I was not going to lose this last table. They were much younger than me. They could take sitting on the ground better."

Lola stared at Hunter and when he raised his eyebrows twice, she burst out laughing all over again.

It did his heart good to know that he was the one bringing joy to her face. He was about to open the basket, but she stopped him.

"Is something wrong?"

"No. Nothing is wrong," she said, still smiling as she opened the basket, took out a small table cloth, and laid the food on the table.

"Well, since you brought the food, the least I can do is serve it up" she explained.

When she held up a little water bottle, she noticed it had bubbles floating in it and it was ice cold.

"Is this what I think it is?"

"What do you think it is?" He asked.

"I think it is a little bottle of Champagne. I could be wrong."

"Yes. It is champagne. I had to be a little inconspicuous. Children are rather nosy at times and the friendly ones will come up and start asking questions if they were to see a bottle that is not a Coke…or a Pepsi."

"Hunter, you think of everything. I love it."

"It's just enough for us to have a cup."

Lola bit into her sandwich.

"Oh my gosh," she exclaimed. "This is so good. Mmh."

"I'm glad you like it. We can thank the deli store that made them, but…" He paused to get her attention.

"To make it taste even better, take a bite of the cheese and wash it down with the champagne."

After swallowing the champagne, closing her eyes, Lola sighed and said, "Oh, Hunter that was so good."

Opening her eyes, his eyes were waiting for hers. There was enough body heat to melt the entire block of cheese on the plate.

Their lips met each other halfway. Children's laughter pulled them apart moments later.

"Should I apologize," he asked in a strained voice.

"No," she said breathless, eating the last of her sandwich. Breaking off a piece of cheese she did as before and washed it down with the last of the champagne.

"How did you hurt your knees?"

"The war." Lola wanted to know more, but just those two words were said in finality.

Maybe one day he will confide in me.

Instead of looking at Hunter, Lola decided it was time to wrap things up. One hour had turned into four.

Her need for Hunter was growing and she hardly knew him. It was definitely not time to throw caution to the wind.

Hunter was sitting leisurely watching her place everything neatly back into the basket.

"Are you ready to go?" He asked.

No, I am not ready to go. I want to spend the rest of my life with you, Lola thought.

"Yes. I need to get ready for work tomorrow."

They were about to get up from the table when someone got Hunter's attention.

"I need to use the restroom. The ladies room is right next to it if you need to go. Care to walk with me?"

"Sure," she said, picnic basket in hand.

Not only the restroom, she thought, as he helped her from the table. *I will go just about anywhere with you, Hunter.*

"Hunter?"

"Yes?"

"Thank you for today. This has to be one of the best days of my life. Friday night comes in right on the tails of today." Before he could reply they were at the restrooms.

"I won't be long. Here, let me have the basket."

"Okay," Lola said, easing her hand from his.

When Lola was safely in the ladies room, Nick pulled Hunter into the bathroom.

"Go get your girl. Right now, Hunter. He is here. I will explain later."

Before Nick could finish his sentence they heard screaming. Hunter was out the door in seconds.

When he entered the ladies bathroom, Lola's blouse was torn and she looked shaken up very badly.

"Lola, baby what's wrong? What happened?"

Staring at Hunter, she was so glad to see him, she burst out crying softly with her hands to her face.

"There was a man, and he…he,"

He rushed to her and held her close.

"It's okay, baby. I am here. I got you," he said, as he gently walked her outside. She was shaking so badly he never wanted to let her go.

One thing he did know just as sure as he was breathing, he was going to tell her everything *this* night.

He loved her too much to have this secret hanging over their heads. Someone wanted to harm his baby and that was not happening.

Hunter spotted Nick who whispered for him to go now.

"Let me have the keys to your car, Lola."

Reaching in her purse for her keys, when she was about to hand them to him, she dropped them.

"Okay," Hunter said lovingly, "that's it. You are in no condition to drive home tonight. Do you have a friend or family I can take you to tonight?"

"Hunter, I think I will be okay. It was just the shock of that man grabbing me and trying to pull me out the window."

When she finished talking a car raised its motor loudly and Lola jumped so badly, Hunter held her tightly in his arms.

"That's it," he said lovingly but sternly. "I am driving you home."

In his car he turned and asked, "Give me a person's number that you trust and I will call and let you speak with them. You can trust me, baby."

She gave him Anna's number.

When the phone began to ring he handed the phone to Lola.

"Anna, can I stay with you tonight?"

"Lola you know you can stay with me…day or night"

Getting suspicious of the call she asked, "What is it? Lola what is wrong. Did Hunter hurt you? You don't sound like my Lola. If he hurt you I swear I will…"

"Stop, Anna. Hunter did not hurt me."

"Well what's wrong?"

Hunter knew he had to get Lola away from here and they were wasting time.

He eased the phone from her hand.

"Anna, this is Hunter, Lola's friend. Give me your address, I'm bringing Lola over."

"Why did that man attack me?" Lola asked, holding her blouse where a few buttons had fallen off in the bathroom.

"I will try to explain everything at your friend's house."

Lola tried to relax with her head back on the head rest. "My car. What…"

"Your car is being moved as we speak."

Smiling, she closed her eyes until they got to Anna's.

At the door Anna said cautiously, "I am letting Lola in here, but not you, mister. I am sorry, but I don't know you like that. Now please leave."

Hunter knew they were sitting ducks as long as they were standing on the porch. He could not afford to cause a ruckus and draw attention.

"Lola, baby. I will see you tomorrow morning," he told her. "Please, you need to go inside. Lock all the doors and don't come out for no one."

Lola quickly spoke up.

"If Hunter can't come in, neither am I."

"But, Lola?" Anna wailed.

"I thought I knew Frank too, but look what he did to me. I mean, you don't really know this man…"

"Hunter, please take me home with you," Lola said as tears began to fall.

Anna quickly pulled Lola inside the door and stood aside for Hunter to follow.

Hunter could barely wait to give Anna a large piece of his mind. He thought Lola would be more comfortable sitting next to her friend, but she sat close to him.

"Anna. Did I get the name right?"

"Yes. You got the name right and…"

"Save your theatrics for someone who cares and is willing to listen to it because right now I don't give a damn."

"Lola doesn't need your childish antics right now. Can't you see? Can't you tell something traumatic has happened to her? Are they making blouses that are torn off the shoulders now…with a button or two missing? Have you even noticed how disheveled her hair is?"

Hunter was so mad he wished now he had taken her to a hotel.

"You know what? I think it would be better if we did leave. If you are a friend, she doesn't need enemies." Hunter stood and reached for Lola's hand.

"Come on, baby. Let's go."

Walking to the door, they stopped when Anna ran to the door and stood in front of it.

"Woman, what is wrong with you?" Hunter asked, holding Lola close to his side.

"Look, I am sorry, okay," she said to Hunter.

"It's just that I have been getting phone calls all evening and when I answer they just hang up."

"Then Lola calls acting all weird and crazy. And to beat all she comes here with a man she met online weeks ago and I don't know if you are making her bring you here and it has just about scared the hell out of me."

"I am pregnant and I have my baby to think about," she said, rubbing her stomach lovingly.

"Lola, if you tell me I can trust this man then I will believe you."

"Yes. You can trust Hunter. He is one of the good guys."

"Now that, that is cleared up. We need to talk…and fast," Hunter said, sitting on the couch in the living room.

"First, congratulations on the baby," Hunter said.

"Thank you."

Before turning to Lola, he prayed to God that she understood what he had to tell her and not to shut him out from her life. Even if it meant losing her, she had to know the truth.

"Lola, I need to tell you something and when you hear this please know that this happened after we met online."

Lola's Spidey senses were doing crazy things to her body.

I knew this was too good to be true, she thought, easing away from Hunter to sit on another chair.

Hunter saw her shutting down completely, but he was not hearing that. Not after what they had shared on Friday night and at the Zoo earlier this afternoon.

"Come here, Lola."

"No. Whatever you have to tell me you can tell me from there."

Hunter stood, walked over and sat down beside her and held her hand. It was a tight squeeze because the chair was for one person. She tried to pull her hand from him, but he held it tighter.

"Let go of my hand, Hunter."

"Lola, sweetheart. I have something to tell you. Please, hear me out before you throw me out."

"Okay. I am listening. You have about ten minutes before I ask you to leave."

You are in danger and…"

"What!" Both women exclaimed.

"Someone wants to hurt you…"

"Why would anybody want to hurt me?"

"Why would someone want to hurt Lola?" Both ladies said simultaneously.

"All I do is go to work and back home. At least most of the time. Sometimes Anna and I go out for a night on the town, but that's it," Lola said, trying harder to pull her hand away. Within seconds she gave up. He was too strong.

Hunter turned to Anna.

"Please stop with the questions. I only have minutes before I am thrown out."

Anna rolled her eyes, folded her hands in her lap and waited.

He turned towards Lola.

5

"Lola, someone paid my firm an excessive amount of money for your protection. We don't know who paid the money and we don't know why. But what we do know is that whoever is trying to hurt you is serious and very dangerous."

"Is that why you have been wining and dining me? Taking me to fancy restaurants?"

When his hand relaxed she tore her hand from his and jumped up from the couch.

"The fun you must have had at my expense. Oh, what a fool I have been."

Lola wanted to go somewhere and shrivel up and die of shame.

She had acted a fool and fallen head over heels in love with this man and he had made a complete and utter fool out of her.

"Mister, you need to leave. Right now," Anna almost shouted, "before I call the police."

Paying her no mind, his mind was still reeling from Lola's words.

Of all the things I just told her, that is what registered in her mind? He thought. *This is not happening. Not today.*

He got up from the couch and slowly walked to Lola.

Heart pounding, she didn't need this man nowhere near her. Her heart was owned by this man and she had been a fool long enough.

She swiftly ran around the couch and stood behind Anna.

Hunter almost burst out laughing but had to catch himself quickly.

If the situation had been less serious he knew he would have probably been on the floor shaking from laughter. What a woman. Sobering up, he stood next to her.

Lifting her chin softly, very calmly, he explained.

"I am not leaving here tonight before we come to an understanding. I promise I will not hurt you and I will do all in my power to honor that promise."

"I care a great deal for you. If you let me I will explain as much as I know, but you have to trust me. My team and I are working to catch this person before he can get to you. He came very close this afternoon in the ladies room at the zoo."

"What do you mean at the zoo?" Anna asked, jumping up from the couch, turning to look at Lola and shoot daggers at Hunter with her eyes.

"Lola, did something happen at the zoo?"

I really can't stand this friend of Lola's any longer, Hunter thought. *Did she not see how she looked when she came here?*

"Look, why don't you explain what happened this afternoon to your friend. My ten minutes are up and you need your rest. I have to go, but Lola, baby if you need me please call me."

He turned to Anna.

"Those telephone calls could be related to what is happening to Lola. Will it be okay if I come by your office tomorrow and ask you about them?"

"I really don't see what they have to do with Lola. I mean, they were probably just some stupid kids playing pranks…"

Hunter sighed deeply, trying not to say something that would hurt Lola's friend.

"Have kids played this kind of prank on you before?"

"Well no, but…"

"I will ask you again. Will it…"

"Yes." Anna paused.

"Yes. I go to lunch around eleven o'clock. Will it be okay if I bring someone with me?"

"Sure. You can even record our conversation if you like. Take pictures for all I care. I just want Lola safe."

Hunter turned to leave, but stopped when he remembered something Anna said.

"Who is Frank?"

"My worst nightmare. Someone I hate more than life itself. And no, I don't want to talk about him right now."

"Be prepared to talk about him tomorrow," Hunter said walking to the door.

Lola held his hand gently and stopped him.

"Do you really have to go?" Lola asked.

"Yes. I need to have a talk with my team." Hunter stared her in the eyes and said, "Walk with me to the door."

Lola continued to hold his hand as they walked to the door.

At the door he held her close and whispered, "I am not playing games with you. I hope you know that kiss at the zoo was very real."

"I'm glad."

"Why?" He asked, smoothing her hair down.

"Because when I kissed you back mine was very real as well." She laid her head on his shoulder and his cologne filled her nostrils making her dizzy with need for this man.

"I'm sorry."

"For what?" He asked, holding her closer.

"Shouting at you in front of…"

Anna's name never crossed her lips. Covering her lips with his, he kissed her softly.

He could barely contain the passion streaming from her body. It was being transmitted to his body head on, but he knew this was not the time.

"Hunter?" She whispered.

"Yes?" he sighed, burying his head in her neck.

"Don't go."

"I have to, baby," he breathed heavily as they strained to hold each other tighter.

"Am I holding you too tight?" He asked.

"No," she sighed, seeking his lips again, never intending to let them go.

Hunter moaned in pleasure. He knew she was the one from the start, but now he was totally certain of it and he was not going to take advantage of her fright earlier to claim her body.

"Lola?"

"Hmm?"

"Baby, I have to go. I will be here early in the morning. Okay?"

"Hunter," she sighed. "Please."

"I really need to be going, baby. I won't be at ease until you are safe."

"Please stay," she sighed heavily as she stared at him holding him closer.

"I would feel so much safer if you stayed. I think Anna wanted you to stay as well, she just didn't know how to ask."

Hunter was about to tell her he couldn't stay when Lola melded her lower body to his…moving passionately against him.

Please, baby," she sighed, "don't go."

"Lola, baby. What you are doing is not fair," he whispered, trying to contain his passions for this woman.

"Hunter. What is that?" She whispered in his ear.

"Lola, sweetheart…" She stopped his words with her body straining to his more sensually.

In defeat…"Yes. Yes," he groaned, holding her so tight she almost cried out from the passion.

"Yes what?" She whispered.

"I'll stay."

"Thank you."

She took his hand and led him to the bedroom she always slept in when she stayed over.

Once the door was closed, he held her gently, "What you did to me downstairs was not fair," he said, smiling. "I think you already know what you do to me."

"Well, don't ever put that much of you on display again if you don't want it toyed with, Mr. Nichols."

Hunter threw his head back laughing boisterously.

"Oh, Lola. You are so good for me," he said, pulling her back into his arms.

"I will take a quick shower then you can use the bathroom."

"Take your time. I'm not going anywhere."

When she came from the shower, she was talking but no one answered.

"Thank you again for staying over, Hunter," she said, smiling looking around.

"Oh, no he didn't."

She found him downstairs on the couch. As much as she wanted him, he was sleeping so peacefully she didn't have the heart to wake him. Instead, she leaned over him and gave him a kiss on the lips.

"Goodnight, Hunter. Sleep well."

Hunter breathed a huge sigh of relief when she was back upstairs.

I love you, baby and I want you badly, he thought, *but tonight is not the time.*

Pretending to be asleep while she kissed his lips had almost done him in. *This is going to be a long night,* he thought, turning on the couch trying to get more comfortable.

Sleep well, my love because you made certain I will not sleep at all.

"You gotta come out sometime," the man said menacing outside of Anna's home.

"You kissed my Lola at the zoo and for that alone I am going to kill you. I almost had her in that bathroom, but you got in the way… again."

Opening a bottle of Pepsi he took it down without taking it from his mouth, spilling a lot of it as he drank.

"I am going to stay here all night if I have to," he said, laying his head back on the headrest.

Waking from a quick nap, when he saw all the lights were turned off inside the house, he went ballistic on the steering wheel.

Banging on the steering wheel, he started ranting and raving.

"Why didn't you come out?"

The man said madly.

"You better not be having sex with my girl. Lola belongs to me. She has always been mine," he said, tiring himself out from all the energy he used on the steering wheel and beating up on the inside of the car.

Leaning his head back on the head rest, he fumed.

"It took me years to find you again…and no man is going to have you. Only me. Only me, my precious Lola."

Surveying the neighborhood, he slowly eased from the car. Walking carefully to the back of the house, his next step caused the security lights to come on.

Hunter was instantly alert.

Unable to sleep after Lola's kiss he had been tossing and turning ever since.

Jumping up he quickly went to the front window and saw nothing.

Rushing to the kitchen he looked out the window and saw a man stooping behind the hedges.

Hunter quickly opened the door and rushed towards the hedges.

Swiftly, the man took off running down the street in the opposite direction. Hunter chased him, but the man was too fast.

Scanning the neighborhood he saw nothing out of the ordinary, turned and went back inside.

Cautious, he listened at Anna's closed bedroom door. All appeared quiet. He then proceeded to Lola's door to check on her.

Thankfully the flood lights didn't wake either woman, he turned to walk back downstairs.

Midway down the stairs, Lola opened her door and saw Hunter walking softly back downstairs.

She quickly followed him.

"Hunter, what were you doing upstairs?"

"I was checking on you and Anna."

"Did checking on us have something to do with the security lights coming on?"

"Yes."

Sitting beside him on the couch, she asked, "Did something happen?"

"Lola. Baby, why don't you go back to sleep. We will talk in the morning."

"Hunter, why did Anna's security lights come on? What are you not telling me?"

"Lola, baby I…"

Lola softly touched his face, smoothing her hand on his jaw.

"Please, don't keep secrets from me, Hunter," Lola said after his hesitation.

"I'm a big girl. I can take it," she whispered, continuing to caress his jaw.

"Okay. I will tell you," he said gently, removing her hand from his jaw.

"Someone was outside the house. I think it was the same person from the zoo this afternoon."

"But, why do they want me? I try to be nice to everyone?"

"I don't know, but I am going to find out. I meant what I said earlier. I will do all that is within me to protect you."

He touched her lower cheek and lifted her face to his. "Do you believe me, baby?"

"Yes. Yes. I do."

"Now to save what little sanity I have left, please go back to bed."

"Save your sanity? Hunter, what are you talking about?"

"Lola. Baby. Take a very good look at what you have on."

When she looked down at her attire, and blushed, he continued.

"Yeah, you should blush," he scolded, gently.

"Goodness, baby, you're wearing next to nothing. I am losing my ability to think and behave in a normal and rational manner because of what you are wearing…or not wearing," he said, running his hand over his hair.

"Sheer curtains cover more than you are covering. Where is your bra? Baby, where is your underwear? I am hanging on to my sanity by a thread. A very weak thread. I can't talk to you anymore with you dressed like that and not want you. Please go back to bed. We can talk in the morning."

Reaching for his hand, although the room was almost dark, the full moon shone brightly through the window. She could tell he was staring at her.

"I'm sorry about my attire. I just rushed down without thinking."

Touching his jaw gently, staring into his eyes, she whispered softly, "Hunter, what if I cut that thread you're hanging on to?"

"Lola. Please, baby. Go back to bed. I truly believe you are still shaken up from earlier. I am probably your hero…for now anyway. Remember we are still in the getting to know each other phase of our relationship. Besides, I am at your friend's home and I don't want to take advantage of that."

"Good night, Hunter," she whispered, kissing him fully on the lips.

Seconds later, he pulled his lips from hers, holding her close, he whispered in her ear.

"I thought you agreed not to wear that perfume again since you know what it does to me."

"I agreed not to wear this perfume when we go on dates," she explained. "This is not a date," she sighed.

"Do you always wear perfume to bed and sleep with next to nothing on?"

"No," she sighed. 'I normally sleep with *nothing* on."

The visions playing havoc in Hunter's mind was making it hard for him to pull away from her, but he was determined not to take advantage of her.

He wanted this relationship to last until they were old and gray and making love this early in the relationship might jinx it. That is until Lola did the unthinkable.

"Oh, Hunter. Sweetheart," she moaned passionately. "I truly hope I have the right to call you that endearment because you got something I want." "Something I need badly," she sighed, throwing all caution to the wind.

Kissing Hunter with all the passion she could muster, he finally took over, drawing her lips and body to him knowing he was not coming back from this passion.

He tried one last time to stop, but when he tried to push her away, she held him close and whispered in his ear, "Please. Hunter, please…sweetheart. Don't push me away."

"Oh, Lola. Baby…" he sighed heavily when she touched him seductively, and whispered, "you have got to stop putting so much of yourself on display."

"I don't mean to, baby, but when you wear next to nothing, and start touching me like you are doing it becomes very hard not to be on display."

Hunter was wondering how they were going to tear themselves away from each other when their need for each other was so great when suddenly a brick came hurling through the window.

Hunter immediately pulled Lola to the floor and covered her.

It took seconds for her mind to right itself from the passion tearing through her.

"I got you, baby. Please don't move," he whispered.

"Hunter, what is going on?"

"I don't know, but someone is not playing around. Stay down, baby. Don't move. I will be back," Hunter said, getting up from covering Lola.

"Hunter?" Lola said, attempting to get up.

"Lola, stay down," he demanded, running to open the door.

Opening the door, he scanned the front yard, but saw no one.

"What is going on down there?" Anna asked from upstairs.

"Anna," Hunter shouted, "stay upstairs. Get back in your room."

"What do you mean get back in my room? What is going on?"

Walking swiftly back to Lola, quickly lifting her from the floor he led her to the stairs and said, "Go upstairs and stay with Anna until I tell you it is safe."

"But what about you?"

"I am okay. I need to check the house and make sure it is safe. Anna, call the police. Lola will fill you in with the details."

In the kitchen he called Nick.

"Yeah, boss?" Nick asked, yawning, glancing at the clock.

"Boss you have got to be kidding me."

"I know it is late, but I need you over here an hour ago. Please apologize to Missy for me."

When he heard the sirens, he went and got the girls from upstairs.

"Anna, please try not to touch anything. After the cops leave we need to talk."

"You damn straight we will have to talk. You come to my house one night and the next thing I know, my living room window and house is trashed."

"For God's sake, Anna," Lola said disgustedly, "give it a rest will you?"

The doorbell chimed and Anna started for the door, but Hunter stopped her.

"I will get it. Stay with Lola."

One police officer wrote down the report from Hunter and Lola since Anna was upstairs sleeping and did not see anything, while the other police walked over to the brick.

Thirty minutes later the police asked if the ladies had someplace they could stay until the window was fixed. Before they could say anything, Hunter spoke up.

"Yes. They have some place to stay."

Anna was about to say something but the look Hunter gave her she closed her mouth and looked down.

"I am sorry ma'am for the disturbance. Due to the threat from the note, we will be driving by for the remainder of the night. In the daytime as well."

"Officer, can I see you outside?" Hunter asked, glancing at Lola.

Thank God she had put on a thick robe when she went upstairs.

"I didn't want to ask you in front of Ms. Wells, but can you tell me what that note said? She is in a lot of danger. I was trying not to bring you guys in on this, but my team, we may have to."

In that moment while he was talking, Nick drove up.

"Actually, Mr. Nichols. The note is for you. Not Ms. Wells. I did not want to alarm the ladies."

"Me!" Hunter exclaimed.

"Look, man. You are not hearing this from me. Read it and ease it back to me before my boss looks this way."

'Stay away from Lola. She is mine. You will die if you don't leave her alone. LOLA IS MINE! Stop kissing on her. Do you hear me?'

"Watch your back, man. That is a pretty woman you are protecting. I had to catch myself from staring at her too long…and I'm married. I don't know what you feel for her, but it seems that beautiful women have a lot of baggage."

"Just because the lady is beautiful does not give anyone the right to harm her, but thanks, man," Hunter said, walking back inside with Nick.

"I will explain all this as soon as I can," he said to Nick.

"Anna I think you need to stay with Lola and me…at least for tonight. Whoever is after Lola knows she is your friend."

"Alright. What do we do? Lola and me. Where are we going?"

Not bothering to answer her, he turned to Lola. "Can you maybe borrow some clothes from Anna? We are definitely not going back to your house. At least not tonight. But, I need you and Anna to go and get the clothes now so we can leave."

Anna was so pissed, she would not go get any clothing.

"You didn't answer my question, Mr. Hunter. Where are we going?"

You will know when we get there, but it is very safe. I know you have the baby to think…"

"If you can't tell me where we are going, then I am not going. I will go to a hotel."

Lola stared at her friend in disbelief before dialing a number on her phone.

"Who are you calling?" Hunter asked Lola.

"I am calling her baby's daddy and we are going to drop her off at his house."

"You will do no such thing. He does not know about the baby."

Lola continued dialing.

"For God's sake, Lola just stop. Hang up the phone," Anna almost screamed to which Lola ignored.

"Hi, Sam. I am sorry to bother you so late, but something happened earlier tonight and I am dropping Anna off at your place. She is a little put out so be warned. Besides, she has something to tell you and it is very important. Okay, bye."

"Lola, how could you? I am not ready to tell Sam about the baby."

"When were you going to tell him, Anna? When the baby is a teenager."

"You are starting to show and look like you are pregnant. I am tired and you keep fussing and talking. Maybe Sam will be able to calm you down. I am done trying."

"I still think she should have gone with us," Hunter said.

"This person or persons are very serious about hurting you and he now knows Anna is your friend."

"Please, Hunter, can we just go," Lola sighed, rubbing her temples at the side of her head.

"I am very tired. Besides when Anna gets like this there is no changing her mind…and she is pregnant. Bad combination."

"Okay. I trust your judgment. She is your friend."

Hunter's friend Nick looked at Hunter.

"And you will not believe the people who are out and about driving at night," he said, frustratingly. "There was a pile up on 240 and…"

"Don't worry about that right now. Man, I'm just glad you're here."

Hunter turned to introduce the two ladies to Nick, but Anna stopped him.

"I have to go upstairs and get some changing…"

"That ship has sailed," Hunter told her maddeningly at his wits end with this woman. "Now let's go."

Anna rushed past Hunter to go upstairs to get some changing clothes and walked into a brick wall. Nick stopped her before she fell back.

"You know it's not polite to walk into strangers," Nick said, on the verge of laughing attempting a little humor.

"Nick? Please," Hunter told him. "Trust me. Now is not the time."

"Sorry boss."

"I am going upstairs to get some clothes," Anna said matter of factly.

"No you are not," Hunter said, dangerously close to telling her something that would no doubt cause Lola to dislike him.

"You had your chance. Now let's go. Sleep in one of Sam's shirt."

Anna stared at Lola for support.

"Let's go, Anna," Lola said calmly.

You heard Hunter."

"Some friend you are," Anna mumbled under her breath.

"Man you weren't kidding about this 240. Traffic is usually not this bad this time of the morning."

Finally exiting the expressway, they sat in silence until they got to Sam's house.

"We won't leave until you are safe inside," Hunter said, walking Anna to the door.

He didn't think she would have gone if Nick escorted her.

Sam locked the door behind her and rushed to Anna. "Baby, what's wrong? What happened? It is two-thirty in the morning."

"It is all Lola's fault," Anna exclaimed.

"I told her not to be dating men online. They are no good and…"

"Whoa! Wait a minute. What in God's name are you talking about? I thought Lola was your best friend. She told us she was going to take it slow and be cautious. Goodness, Anna. All men online are not like Frank. He was just a bad seed from the start. If he wasn't online, he would still be a monster…a bad seed. How can you say it is Lola's fault? Lola loves you."

"Oh, now you are taking her side."

"Anna. Baby. I am not taking no one side. I just thank God you came out of your ordeal with Frank alive. I love you, Anna."

Sam took her hand and led her to the couch.

"Now, I want you to tell me why you had to come over here at this hour?"

When she hesitated, Sam said, "Lola said you had something to tell me and it was very important."

"I don't want to tell you."

"Why?"

"Because you are going to hate me and I don't want you to hate me because I love you too, Sam."

"Just tell me. We will get through it together."

"I'm pregnant."

Taking a deep breath he let it out slowly.

"You're what?"

"I am pregnant. I told you, you would hate me."

"Calm down, Anna. It's just a shock that's all. Especially since you told me you could not have children. I would have been more responsible."

With phone in hand Anna began dialing a number. "What are you doing? Who are you calling at three o'clock in the morning?" Sam asked.

"I'm calling an Uber. I am going to a hotel."

Sam grabbed the phone and threw it hard against the wall.

"Why did you do that?" Anna asked, jumping up from the couch.

"I am not staying here with a man who doesn't want his own child."

"You know something, Anna. As much as I love you, you are about as crazy as they come. I did not tell you I did not want the baby. I did not tell you I did not want you. You are the one who is jumping to conclusions. Can't we sit down and talk about it?"

"Sam, you broke my phone."

"I did. I can buy you another phone, but if you think I was going to let you go out this time of night carrying a child of mine you don't know me that well. How many months are you?"

"Four."

Not skipping a beat, she wailed, "But, Sam. That phone had all my numbers in it. My connections. Everything."

"I think I can retrieve your information, but now I want you to sit down and tell me everything that happened tonight. Why did you need to come over here in the middle of the night? And let's talk about the four months of carrying my child and I did not have a clue."

"Where are we?" Lola asked.

"First I would like you to meet Nick, properly. So much was going on, you and he didn't have a chance to be introduced."

"Nick, Lola. Lola, Nick."

After introductions, Lola sat down waiting for some answers.

Nick sat down by Lola, looked at Hunter and when he nodded, he proceeded to ask Lola some questions.

"Lola, your old boyfriends. Did you have a bad breakup with any of them?"

"No!" She gave a half smile.

"Actually, I haven't had many boyfriends. Not real ones. There was one and we both decided it wasn't going anywhere so we parted ways amicably."

"Well, have you ever made someone mad? On the job? At church? A party? Anywhere."

"No!"

"Well you pissed somebody off enough for them to want to hurt you," Nick continued, baffled.

Lola jumped up from her seat and stared at Hunter. "Is this why you brought me here? To gang up on me?" Throwing up her hands in the air, she started for the door.

"You know, Anna was probably right."

"Talking about me pissing somebody off. You don't have to know someone for them to hate you now-a-days. Hunter, you know that," she said fuming.

"Now will someone please take me to Sam's to be with Anna?"

Hunter rushed to her side. "Lola, baby. We are sorry, but…"

"No buts, Hunter. I told you. I don't know who wants to hurt me. To my knowledge, I have never even met someone I didn't like. Well maybe one, and that was Frank."

Hunter held her by the shoulders until she raised her eyes to his.

"Think, baby. Nick was not trying to be mean. We just need some answers to find out who wants to hurt you."

"Someone had to have crossed your path that you couldn't stand."

"Well," she said, thinking of Frank.

6

"Well what?" Nick asked, gently, coming to stand by her.

"It may not mean much to you, but could be crucial in finding this person or persons who don't like you."

"What is it, Lola?" Hunter asked softly.

"Well, Frank, this guy who almost killed Anna. She met him online. That is why she doesn't like you a lot. She is afraid for me. She thinks you are a bad man Hunter because Frank was so vicious and mean."

Nick and Hunter eyed each other, but said nothing. Hunter led her back to the couch.

"I know you are very tired, but could you please tell us a little about what happened between the two of them. How did he almost kill your friend?"

"He stabbed her with a knife inches from her heart. We tried to warn her about him, but she wouldn't listen."

"What did you warn her about?"

"Well, we would see him with other women and…" Lola hesitated.

"What?" Both men said at the same time.

"We asked Anna not to confront him about having women alone. That he might get mad and hurt her, but she did not listen. When Anna did confront him he started accusing us, her friends, saying that we just wanted to break them up. Although I begged Anna to be careful of him, she would always say that I was jealous of their relationship and she would always give him another chance."

"And were you?" Nick asked, wanting to leave no stones unturned.

"Nick, you are getting on my last nerve. I am trying to like you because of Hunter, but you are making it very hard. I told you. No, I was not jealous. I was actually afraid of the guy."

"Why?" Hunter asked, softly.

"Well, he used to stare at me all the time when Anna wasn't looking. It gave me the creeps. I told Anna about it and she said I was still jealous and wanted the man for myself which was a joke. I could see the evil in his eyes. She did everything for him."

"We continued to warn her, but she would not listen until one day she saw him kissing a woman. They got in the woman's car and Anna followed them to a hotel. She sat in her car for two and a half hours until they came out of the hotel. He kissed this woman before he helped her into her car."

"After Anna cried for a while, she told me she dried her tears and was going to have it out with him later. I begged her not to do that, but she just wouldn't listen. That night she told him she was through and she never wanted to see him again because she had seen him with that woman. She told him to get out of her house and he went berserk."

"The neighbors heard her screaming and called the police. He stabbed her numerous times and would have killed her, but when he heard the sirens, he took off. Anna was rushed to the hospital. He was finally caught and we all breathed a sigh of relief when he went to jail."

"Lola, what is Frank's last name?"

"I think it is Shift. Frank Shift."

Lola noticed the look that passed between the two men.

"What is it?" She asked nervously.

No answer as the men looked down and then stared at her.

"What is it?" She asked again, losing all strength in her body.

Holding her hand comfortably, Hunter said, "Lola, baby, Frank Shift escaped from prison four months ago."

"No, that can't be true. No one told us he escaped. Anna should have been first on the list for them to call. Don't you understand? She is in more danger than me. She is the one that got away."

Lola jumped up and just as quickly sat down when the room started spinning.

"Take it easy, Lola," Hunter said, uneasily.

"No. I can't take it easy. He is probably after Anna. I have got to warn her. We may fuss sometimes, but I love her…and she loves me. Don't you understand," Lola almost screamed, "he wants to kill her and maybe me as well."

Hunter pulled her to him tightly and held her close until she calmed down.

"Nick, call Sam and tell him not to open the door for anyone. I don't care if it is his mother. They can't leave the house for anything."

Dialing Sam's number, Hunter said, "She is pregnant and gets irritated easily. Try and do all the talking to Sam."

"You got it, boss."

"Why has this not been on the news? Why wasn't Anna not told about this?" Lola asked.

"The man was very clever. He killed a laundry worker, got his clothes and drove out the prison without anyone noticing it. He hid the laundry worker where no one would find him until a few days ago. Since the man lived alone and was not married, there was no one to ask about him until a few days ago."

"How is she?" Lola asked Nick when he hung up.

"As well as can be expected. She is terrified, especially since she is pregnant. Before Sam realized, Anna had listened in on the conversation behind his back."

"I need to go to her," Lola said, getting up from the couch. She was determined not to let the look on Hunter's face deter her. Anna needed her and she wanted to be there with her.

"I can't stand it!" Lola cried, walking back and forth, wearing out the carpet.

"I'm the one who should be complaining," Anna said, rubbing her stomach.

"I can go into labor any minute now. We have been in this God forsaken safe house for what, five months."

"Well at least you have Sam in here with you. He was blessed to be able to take a year off and keep his job. Me, I'm here all alone. I can't even call my mom and dad. No one."

"Speaking of no one. Now that you mention it, I have not seen Hunter since the first few nights he stayed here. One day he was here and the next day he was gone. He just up and left us here by ourselves. Has he even called to make sure you're alright?"

"No he has not and I don't want to talk about it," she told Anna when she was about to start asking a lot of questions she was not willing to answer right now.

"So he does not know about the baby you are carrying for him," Anna asked, seriously.

"No, Anna. He does not know and he is never going to know."

"But, Lola…"

"Don't you dare but me, Anna," Lola said, heatedly. "If you could have seen the look on Hunter's face when he walked away from me that morning, I could have died. I vowed that morning I never wanted to see that look on his face again. I died inside that morning."

"Lola, please sit down and let's talk about it."

"I told you, Anna, I don't want to talk about it."

"Well, Lola, you are going to talk about it. I have let you mope, cry, and get angry…even take it out on me, but not anymore."

"What you are doing is not healthy for the baby nor you. That baby has done nothing wrong and the way you are mistreating your body is a crying shame. Now sit your bottom down and let's talk it out."

Lola stared at Anna and realized she had been treating her body very badly. If Hunter did not want the baby then neither did she, she had thought at the time.

Lola stared at Anna and burst out crying profusely sitting heavily on the couch.

As fast as she could waddle, Anna sat down and comforted Lola as best she could.

"Come on, Lola. Honey, all that crying isn't doing the baby any good either. It is going to be alright. You are going to have to tell Hunter about the baby. Honey, he has a right to know."

"He does not have a right to know," Lola said, wiping her tears.

"He hates me, Anna and it is all my fault."

"Well, it couldn't have been all your fault. I mean, a woman does not get pregnant all by herself."

"But you don't understand, Anna. Hunter did not want to have sex. As much as he loved me, he never wanted to take advantage of me."

"I kind of seduced him. I loved him so much and I wanted to be with him that night so I did things to his body and I knew he was not going to be able to hold out. That next morning, he left and I have not seen him since."

"Wow! You mean my Lola, who always was so level headed seduced a man that left you with a baby. I never thought I would see the day. And you got on me for sleeping with Frank."

"Anna, you slept with Frank the first week you met him. You let the man in your home after one Zoom chat. You gave him money. You paid for everything."

"Okay, Lola. Okay, I get it. Maybe Hunter is not quite as bad as Frank, but…"

"But, nothing!" Lola almost shouted at her friend. "Hunter is not trying to stab and kill me like Frank was trying to do to you. You can't even put Frank and Hunter on the same planet. Hunter will always be a man. A good man who would never hurt a hair on my head."

"I know he would want to take responsibility for the baby, but if Hunter wants to marry me just because I'm carrying his child, I won't do that to him. I will never trick him to marry me just because I got pregnant. I will raise the baby alone first. So don't you ever put Frank and Hunter's name in the same sentence again…ever."

"Goodness, Lola. I'm sorry. I didn't mean nothing by it. I thought you said you did not want the baby."

"Anna, don't you know me at all? I want this baby so badly it hurts. Don't you get it? Hunter. The man I will love forever gave me this precious gift. I was hurt," she explained, rubbing her stomach.

"I know I need to eat better. I was in my feelings, but not anymore."

"So, you honestly are not going to tell him about the baby?"

Smiling as she lovingly massaged her stomach, "No. It would not be fair."

"But, Lola. You are the one who told me to tell Sam about his baby and now you are saying you are not going to tell Hunter. That is so hypocritical. And it is not fair to Hunter."

"I know you are right. Now that the shoe is on my foot, it does not fit as well. It was different with you and Sam. Sam loves you."

"My pregnancy is different. You and Sam loves each other. I want to tell Hunter so badly, but if he rejects me, I think I would die. I intend to leave after you have your baby."

"But, Lola. You can't. Sam talked to Nick yesterday and he said they would have Frank in custody later this week."

"Are you sure Sam is not going to tell Nick and Hunter about my baby?"

"I told him if he told either one about you having a baby, I would run away with his baby and he would never find us."

Lola burst out laughing. "What did he say to that?"

"He laughed at me until he realized I was serious. He then promised me he wouldn't tell."

Lola was playing with the tassels on the end of one of the pillows on the couch with a faraway look on her face.

"Lola?"

Anna waved a hand in front of her friend's face to get her attention.

"Earth to Lola."

Lola jumped and looked at Anna guiltily.

"What is it? Why are you so spaced out?"

"There is something else I need to tell you. I haven't been completely honest with you about that night Hunter and I made love."

"What is it? You know I have your back."

"I was a virgin that night. I had never gone all the way with a man. I didn't tell Hunter because if he had known he would have stopped and I didn't want him to stop. When he first entered me, he didn't know to be gentle. I had gotten him so worked up with what I was doing to his body he came at me full throttle. It hurt so badly I kinda screamed too loud from the pain it caused and he stopped immediately."

Anna was sitting up in her chair as if she was watching a movie.

"Girl, I swear all I need is some buttery popcorn. What happened next?"

"He was about to lift from me, and I started crying. He gently eased from me and pulled me in his arms and held me until I stopped crying."

"He started apologizing saying how sorry he was for taking advantage of me. He said if he had known I was a virgin he never would have even tried to make love to me. I knew if I let him leave after that, he would never touch me again."

Lola was reminiscing in her mind about that night.

"Lola," Anna almost screamed, "what happened after that?"

"I gently started touching him telling him it was okay and that I had led him on. I softly kissed him, and asked him to forgive me. I continued caressing him until he was fully aroused again."

"Anna it was so sweet and so sensual. We didn't talk, he just let me have my way with him."

"After minutes of me gently caressing him, he rolled over to me, held me in his arms lovingly and said gently, "I am going to make it up to you. The hurt and pain I caused you. I didn't know you were a virgin, sweetheart. I am so sorry.""

"That man was talking so smooth saying he was going to kiss the hurt away. By the time he kissed the hurt away, I wanted him so badly, total ecstasy had taken over my entire body. When he whispered and told me he was not going to hurt me, I lost all dignity known to women."

Lola looked at Anna, eyes glowing with love and said, "I don't think I have to tell you more. If you put two and two together, I think you should come up with one-hundred and two. That is how powerful our making love was that night. He was so sweet, and so loving, before the night was over, I knew every inch of his body…and he knew mine."

"Oh, Lola. That is so beautiful. Hunter left a part of that love with you. I love it. Don't take that joy away from him, Lola. Please. I really think he will understand."

"Don't you see, Anna? What we shared was so all consuming and so powerful, I won't be able to take it if he walks away from me and the baby."

"Well, I hope you change your mind."

"I love you, girl," Lola said, walking to the kitchen to get a glass of milk.

"I love you too, Lola."

Lola nearly dropped her glass when she heard a loud piercing scream coming from the sitting room. Rushing into the sitting room she saw Anna's face contorted in excruciating pain.

"Oh, Anna, you're in labor."

She quickly called Sam from the basement.

"Do you still love her?" Nick asked, cautiously. Since that last night Hunter and Lola had been together, Hunter had been in a funk Nick had never seen before. Knowing Hunter for twenty some years he had always kept a level head and never lost it with a woman.

"Who said anything about love?" He asked Nick.

"Come on, man," Nick said.

"Man I know you and you have not been the same since you left that morning. It is okay to say you love her. I know you love her, Hunter. You told me months ago that you love her."

"I told you I never want to see her again or hear her name again. Once we put Mr. Shift back behind bars she can drop off the face of the planet for all I care."

"I know you don't mean that so why are you against her? All she did was show you how much she loved you. You didn't have to take the bait if you did not want it."

"Stop blaming Lola for everything. You know you enjoyed her. I am a witness to how much you enjoyed that night. At least I heard how much you enjoyed yourself. I have never heard you lose it like you did that night. And I know these walls are not that thin, but I still had to sleep in the car."

"I'm sorry, man. I didn't know I was that loud. I tried to be quiet, but…"

Nick laughed. "It wasn't just you. Trust me. You both got lost in each other."

Nick thought long and hard before he asked the next question, but knew it had to be asked.

"Did you all use protection that night?"

"Man, don't be asking me questions like that. No, I did not use protection. Since she was so amorous, I assumed she was on the pill. I mean, the way she came at me, she had to be prepared. She used me, man. I almost hate her for that."

"If I didn't know you so well, I would not say what I am about to say."

"Nick, I told you to drop it. I don't want to hear about that woman. She used me, man."

"How many times did she use you, Hunter?"

"What?"

"You heard me. How many times did Lola use you? I mean you say she used you. I guess after that first time she used you, in shame you quietly left the room and had nothing else to do with her."

"I told you to…"

"I know what you told me and I also know that you did not leave that room until daybreak. You could have left anytime you wanted to."

"So stop blaming Lola for something you enjoyed more than you have enjoyed a woman in your life. I know you, Hunter. I have seen you with women and no woman has ever gotten under your skin like Ms. Wells. What if you got her pregnant? Man you have been acting weird lately and that is not you, man. You are snapping at us guys if we look your way for more than a second. And, God forbid if we say her name."

"She was a virgin and I didn't know it. I hurt her, Nick."

Nick whistled. "Why didn't she tell you before you…well before you? I think you know what I am trying to say."

"I asked her that and she said because she knew I would have stopped and she didn't want me to stop."

Nick looked at Hunter and smiled humorously.

"Man this no laughing matter. She should have told me."

"Soo, when you found out she was a virgin how fast did you run from the room?"

"What?"

"When she told you she was a virgin, how long did it take you to leave the room? Since you were so mad at her for not telling you she was a *virgin*."

"Look man, it was complicated."

"But not so complicated that you never left the room. Not so complicated that you did not leave her room until the next morning."

"Not so complicated that you let her use you even after you found out that she was a virgin. Not so complicated that it did not stop you from moaning, and groaning in a frenzy, you hollered out so loud one time I went and slept in the car."

"Not so complicated that you had her near screaming and muttering words of no consequence from what you were doing to her. I am a little confused as to who was using whom."

"Alright. I get it okay. What we shared was so deep and so intense and so out of this world fulfilling that it scared the hell out of me. It was as if our bodies exploded into the universe…together."

"It's like a part of her is still inside me."

When Hunter finished Nick started laughing.

"Man, you are so whipped," Nick said through his laughter.

"Ms. Wells has you by the balls so tight, you don't know your head from your feet. Man, you don't hate Lola. You hate the power she has over you. You hate the fact that you couldn't get enough of her. Admit it, man. You love her. Plain and simple."

Hunter stared at Nick before he got up and walked from the room. He had to think.

Dear God, what if I got her pregnant? A little me could be growing inside her right now. My little baby. Our little baby that we made together…from love.

He knew that now.

He knew why he couldn't leave her that night after just one time. Even after he found out she was a virgin. Knowing he was the first to show her love had unleashed feelings of such powerful force, he had reached for her all through the night.

I needed her more than life that night. Three times had not been enough. I barely gave her time to come to her senses before I was on her again. Nick was right, he admitted as his thoughts continued to ravish his mind.

Lola had been honest with her feelings. She had needed me that night. Needed my closeness. My protection. My understanding. She had not used me.

She had expressed her true feelings she had for me and I had taken and taken all night long. She had been the first to touch me and rock my world with her gentle touches.

I had woken her from sleep many times and she had been so loving and kind and giving.

Never complaining. If she was sore, and she had to have been, the many times I had turned to her. She would silently wrap me in her arms and hold me close to her heart. Her passion had ran deep as she had loved me unconditionally.

"Oh, Lola. Baby I have been so wrong. So selfish. God please forgive me. I will make it right. Even if she is not carrying my baby, I hope to have many with her one day when we marry. If she will still have me."

Hunter rushed back into the room as Nick got off the phone. "What's wrong?"

"Anna went into labor yesterday. She and Sam have a little boy."

"What do you mean, yesterday? They were supposed to tell us the day she went into labor so we could be there."

The look on Nick's face was troubling.

"What is it?" Hunter almost shouted.

"Mr. Shift tricked the cops again. He is still on the loose. The man is smart. We would have had him, but they wanted the glory when he got caught so they put us off the case. I am sorry man. We better get to the safe house and check on everyone."

"You were right," Hunter said, as Nick drove along to the safe house.

"About what?" Nick asked.

"I do love Lola. Very much. She may have come on to me first, but I was a very willing participant. She is the only woman I have completely lost it with."

"It scares me what she bring out in me when we make love. If she is carrying my baby, I would be the happiest man alive. Nick, can you drive a little faster? I need to see her. I have been a fool. All this wasted time we could have been together."

"Well, at least now you can tell her how you truly feel and the two of you can talk out your feelings."

"We don't have to talk about our feelings. We showed each other our true feelings, all night long. I just didn't want to admit that a woman had that much power over me."

"She only had to touch me and my body lit up like lightening striking in the night sky. I know she loves me and I love her. That is what she was telling me that night."

"That she loved me. She told me over and over again, but I was so selfish I took and took. All night long."

"We will be there in five minutes."

Inside the safe house all Hunter wanted to see was Lola and her beautiful smile. To wrap her in his arms and never let her go. Tell her he was sorry for his terrible attitude that following morning.

One look at the couple, he knew something was very wrong.

"Anna, where is Lola?"

"I am sorry, Hunter, but Lola left."

Hunter's world came crashing down around him. The room was spinning. His body was shutting down. His entire being was morphing into someone else.

"What do you mean, she left?" Nick asked, wanting to shake her and Sam within an inch of their lives. Thank God they had the baby between them.

He stared at them as they sat there all lovey dovey with their little baby in their arms without a care about the danger Lola could be in.

Nick glanced at Hunter and knew he was crashing.

Taking matters into his hands, he got on the phone and called every man on the team.

"If it is not a matter of life and death, drop everything you are doing and meet us at the spot. NOW!!!

Hunter was ready to tear into Anna and Sam.

"Anna, you had better tell us something or we are going to take that baby of yours and keep it until you tell us what you know about Lola leaving this safe house. And if you don't know anything, you better make up something that is very convincing."

"Now wait just a minute," Sam said, getting up from the couch prepared to defend his family, but Hunter had reached his limit on patience.

Lola could be in dire danger every second they did nothing, he thought.

But by the grace of God that kept Hunter from hitting Sam. Instead, taking a few deep breaths, "Nick, get the baby and take him away."

"Okay!" Sam and Anna said at the same time when Nick was about to take the baby.

"Start talking," Hunter hissed furiously.

"Lola said she did not want to be here when you came because you hated her."

"Where is Lola, Anna? I will not ask you again," Hunter exclaimed dangerously.

"She said she was going to her house to pack and leave. She wanted to get a few things for the baby…"

"Baby?" Hunter exclaimed, his body losing strength.

Anna looked at Sam holding the baby close to her. *Oh, God, I let my dear Lola leave and I did nothing to stop her,* Anna thought sadly.

"You let Lola leave this safe house pregnant with a baby knowing she was putting herself and the baby in danger and you never thought to tell me?"

"Hunter, I am so sorry. Lola said she didn't want you to know about…"

"Cut the crap, Anna. My God, but she and the baby better be alright."

"Gabe, it's me. Get to Lola's house ASAP. Forget the Spot. Run all sirens, but cut them when you get closer to her house. We are on our way," Nick said as he and Hunter rushed from the safe house.

"If something happens to Lola, do you think Hunter will be back here?" Anna asked, looking down at the precious baby in her arms.

"I know he will," Sam said.

"Should we try and make a run for it? Get in the car and drive until we think it is safe?" She asked.

"I don't think there is a place on earth where we can run and he not find us. Let's just pray that he finds Lola and the baby alive and well. If not, we won't have the life as we know it now. I didn't know he loved her as much as he does. The man was livid."

Sam smiled at his son and whispered, "I understand Hunter. I love my son already and will do everything in my power to protect him…and you, Anna."

Anna held her baby close and laid her head on Sam's shoulder, praying that everything would turn out alright.

"I know, Sam. I know."

Lola packed a few things in haste. She didn't want to stay too long not knowing where danger lies.

"It's just you and me, kid," she said, massaging her stomach lovingly.

"I am going to tell you all about your wonderful daddy and how he is the best man on the planet. But we will talk later cause' mommy really needs to be going now."

Lifting the bag, she turned to leave and fell back to the floor, fear freezing her limbs.

"Well, well, well. I see that you do remember me. But tell me this, Ms. Lola, love of my life. Did you not think I wouldn't find you?"

Taking deep breaths, Lola couldn't move. Fear had her glued to the floor.

The images in her mind was Anna being stabbed over and over again by this man.

Trying very hard not to show fear she slowly got up from the floor and sat on the bed. Anything to keep her away from this man.

"Frank? What do you want? I thought you were in jail."

"Jail could not keep me away from you. I told you I would take care of you and I meant that."

"You mean Anna. You were dating Anna. I am sorry about how things…"

"Stop it, Lola. You are trying to make me mad, but I don't want to…unless you make me."

"But, I don't understand. What do you want with me? I didn't know you until you started dating Anna."

"My dear, Lola. You need a spanking. How soon do we forget? You told me over and over that you would love me always. You made me so happy with those words, I pushed you higher and higher on the swing. You would laugh and laugh. You were so happy when I pushed you on that swing."

He saw recognition in her eyes.

"Now you get it," he said slowly.

"Franklin is that you? We were kids playing on the swings. We used to play all the time because there were no children around but us. But we were just kids trying to help each other get by. I did love you, but not love you like a woman loves a man."

"Stand up, Lola," he said, meanly.

He is going to know that I am pregnant now that I am showing a little, she thought.

Lord please don't let him hurt my baby. This is the most precious thing I own in the world.

"I said stand up. Don't let me have to tell you again."

Lola slowly stood up as his eyes focused on her lovely face. When they traveled down her body to her belly, his entire countenance changed.

His breathing was becoming erratic. He slowly eased a knife from his waist and started hitting himself with it on the thigh.

Walking to her slowly he caressed her face.

"What made me so mad at you was the fact that you did not recognize me when I started dating your friend. I would stare at you all the time hoping to jog your memory of the love we have for each other."

"Frank…"

"Don't you dare call me Frank. I am and always will be Franklin to you. You hear me?"

"I'm sorry, Franklin."

To hear her say his name he breathed in and out passionately.

"Say my name again," he whispered.

"Franklin, listen."

Putting a finger to his lips, he wanted her to be quiet as he feasted on her use of his name.

"What is making me so angry now is the fact that you have been a very bad girl. Did you really break our vows and lie with another man? Is that a baby I see growing in your belly?"

Straightening her back, Lola stood tall and said, "You slept with my best friend right in front of me and you talk to me about breaking vows. How dare you?"

7

"When I laid with your stupid friend, it was you I was thinking about. I was trying to make you jealous. Oh, Lola my darling. We can finally be together and no one will be able to stop us."

"I was very smart. I came to live here knowing no one would bother looking here. Took me a while to get past that stupid code on your alarm system. I even slept in our bed. Now we can be together. I have money. You don't have to work, baby. I will take care of you."

Lola thought she would die on the spot. The stench that came from him was horrible.

I have two baths in this house and he never thought to take a bath, she thought.

"Frank, I never loved you in that way. We were childhood kids playing on the swings at the playground. Remember? We never said anything about love. We were only kids."

Frank slapped her hard across the face, knocking her back on the bed, looked at her and smiled crazily.

"See what you made me do. Frank is not my name. Your friend could not call me Franklin. That was reserved for you and you only. For the last time it is Franklin."

"I'm sorry, Franklin," she said, thinking about her baby. *Oh, God how I love this baby*, she thought. *Please don't let this man hurt my baby.*

Tears began to form on her lids, but she quickly let them dry in case he wanted to touch her again and try to console her.

"We were more than just childhood kids playing together. I told you I would always take care of you and be there for you. Don't you remember?"

"Yes. I remember, but I thought you were playing. You know…like a game. Games children play."

"Well, it was not a game to me. Especially since you were promised to me. Now I have a pretty good idea who the man was that put that baby in your stomach, but it has got to go."

"No man gives you what I am going to give you. When we take that baby out, I will put one in you and we can raise him and love him. Together. Just you and me."

"You are not taking my baby," she said, backing away from him.

Forget trying to appease this lunatic, she thought. *He is not going to listen.*

"But that is not my baby. I am going to kill the man that thought he could give you one before me. I told you I would take care…"

Lola was going to fend for her child come hell or high water.

If I never see Hunter again, I have this precious little baby and I aim to keep him, she thought, looking around the room to see what she could throw at him or hit him with.

"And I am telling you that you are not taking this baby from me. I love the man that gave me this baby with all my heart. There will be no other man for me. I gave myself to him willingly…"

"Shut up!" He hissed, menacingly.

"Shut up, I say. You love me. You love me," he continued to scream, walking slowly to her.

"I had to sleep with that fool friend of yours just to get next to you and now you say you don't love me."

Lola decided to be honest. This man was already delusional. He was not going to listen rationally.

"No, Frank, I don't love you. I love someone else. I love this baby's daddy."

"No you don't love him," he shouted madly.

"You love me. And, for the last time, my name is not Frank. It is Franklin. Franklin. You hear me?"

Paying him no mind, she picked up the lamp from the night stand and threw it at him. Direct hit.

"Yes!" She whispered as he fell to the floor.

"Lola. Now you have made me mad. I am going to cut that baby from you and give you mine," he said, trying to get up from the floor.

"He promised me he would give you to me."

With all her strength she pushed past him, but not before he was able to cut one of her legs with the knife he pulled from his pants.

Lola hollered out in pain, but continued to run down the stairs hoping to make it to the front door. He shakily got up from the floor and ran after her.

"I'll get you, you hear me. You are mine," he shouted madly seconds behind her.

"I escaped jail so we could be together. And if I can't have you," he raged, "he certainly won't have you. Thought he could fool me. Maybe you, but not me."

Lola was seconds from the front door when a hand grabbed her hair and yanked her back into his chest.

Lola screamed and fought the best she could, but losing blood from her leg and tired from stress, her strength was fading fast.

"Guys that is my life in that house. Please be careful. She is pregnant with my baby," Hunter said, sick inside, wondering if he would ever be the same again.

"I am parking on the street behind her house."

Hunter rushed from the car before it stopped, paying no heed to Nick's warning to be careful.

"We are in place, boss and we have eyes on the inside. The woman and man are in the main bedroom on the top floor. He is unraveling as we speak. You need to get in there now," Gabe told Hunter.

"She threw a lamp at him and he is not happy about it."

Getting in was not as easy as Hunter had thought. Lola not only had a top notch alarm system. She had good wood structure.

After seconds, but what seemed like hours to Hunter, finally inside, he saw what was happening in slow motion. Lola had made it down stairs and although he was hopping, the man was catching up with her.

Frank was running behind her. Her movements were slowing down giving Frank the chance to catch up to her.

He saw Frank pull her hair so hard it caused her to crash into his chest. Lola screamed in pain.

Hunter wondered if his heart would give out. Frank was holding Lola so close to him, Hunter knew if he shot the wrong way the bullet could still hit her.

"I told you I will take care of you, but no, you had to go and mess up my plans. If I can't have you, that crazy buffoon who gave you that baby won't have you either," he hissed savagely, raising his arm with the knife.

Lola tried to wrestle away from him, but he was too strong.

"Be still or else I will snap your pretty little neck. You won't get away from me this time. He thought he could play me, but I found you first. You hear me? I found you first!" he shouted viciously.

"Oh, God! Please," Hunter choked, aiming his gun. Lola was so close to Frank, Hunter had to be careful of his aim. *My son or daughter's life is at stake.*

In the split second it took for him to react, he saw Frank grip her better to stab her in the stomach. Raising the gun to shoot Frank, Hunter's body froze. He couldn't move.

What if I shoot Lola, he thought in terror.

"Lola," Hunter screamed.

Stopping the knife before it got to her stomach, Frank instantly recognized that voice.

Wanting Hunter to see the woman he loved get stabbed with his baby inside her, he quickly turned Lola to Hunter. Holding the knife to her stomach, Frank laughed insanely with glazed eyes at the victory he felt.

"She is not yours. She is mine. You hear me," he shouted at Hunter.

"You touched her. You had no right to touch her. She is mine. Always has been. He lied to me," he hissed, raising his hand in the air, but before he could puncture her stomach, he fell to the floor in a dead heap.

Hunter noticed one of his men to the left of him had made the shot. Weak in the knees, he dropped to the floor until he saw Lola being pulled down with Frank because his arm was still around her. Before she hit the floor he was there to pull her from Frank's lifeless arm.

"Lola. Baby can you hear me?" He asked, holding her close, never wanting to let her go. "I love you, baby. Can you hear me?"

"Hunter," she whispered, "I knew you were coming. I love you."

Laying her head on his chest she passed out. It was then he noticed the blood running on the floor. Thinking she was losing his baby, he gave a loud wail before the paramedics came to take her away.

"Go away," he shouted, holding her close to his heart, not letting her go. "Leave her alone. Leave my baby alone."

Nick and Gabe came and prized his arms from around her.

"She is alive, Hunter," Nick explained.

"She just passed out, but she needs emergency care. She is losing too much blood. Let the paramedics do their job."

Safe in the ambulance, the paramedics spoke with Nick and Gabe.

"We don't think it is wise for Mr. Nichols to go in the ambulance with the young lady. He will only be in the way," the paramedic explained to Nick and the boys.

"We will let you tell him he can't ride with her, but the man won't be responsible for his actions. He thinks she has lost his precious baby."

The paramedic turned to Hunter, "Sir you are welcome to ride in the ambulance."

"I froze," Hunter stated irritably. "The woman I love. Her life and the life of my baby was at stake and I froze. I will never forgive myself. I mean, what if you guys had not been there. What if…"

At the hospital, Hunter was a mess. He was in agony that he did not take the shot. His men tried to make him see reason.

"Listen, boss. If you had made that shot you very well could have hit Lola. Frank had her glued to his body. Man, forget the should've, could've and the would've. Just be thankful we were there. We actually got a better shot than you ever could," Nick reasoned.

"I know, but what…"

"Let it go, man. Frank turned Lola to you so you could see her face when he struck her stomach. You could not have taken that shot."

"Hopefully, now you see why we don't let families get involved in these cases. Your emotions were all over the place. Man, you were way too close to the situation from the start. Thank God she is alive and leave it at that."

Sitting down, he put his head in his hands and began taking deep breaths to calm down. He conceded that Nick was right and he needed to be thankful.

He still refused to take Anna or Sam's phone calls or speak with them. They would be off his friends list forever.

It was agony waiting for the doctor to come and give them some news. Forty minutes later Hunter thought he was literally going to explode, when the doctor finally came through the door.

All the men sat at attention, but Hunter rushed to the doctor for news.

"Ms. Wells is going to be just fine. The wound on her leg was cut deeper than we first realized and she lost a lot of blood, but she is going to be okay."

Hunter dreaded asking the one question that would change his life forever. "Doctor is the baby…" Is the baby…?"

He couldn't get the rest of it out. It appeared all hope was lost.

"The babies are fine. They were never in any danger. It was the mother we were worried about."

"You said babies?" Hunter asked, heart pounding.

"Yes. Ms. Wells is having twins."

Hunter slumped into a chair, put his head in his hand and cried softly.

His men rushed to his side. Nick rubbed his back and soothed him, handing him a handkerchief to dry his eyes.

"It's okay, man," his men consoled. "You have been through a lot."

"When can I see her?" He asked the doctor.

"She will be in a room soon. The nurse will come and get you when she is comfortable."

"Thank you, doctor."

When the doctor left, the men sat next to him and tried to cheer him up.

"Dang, man. You knocked the ball out of the park on the first hit. Twins. Congratulations, man."

His cell phone rang. Checking the caller, he frowned and put it back in his pocket.

Nick watched Hunter closely, perceiving who the caller had been.

"Hunter? Boss."

"Yeah, man. What is it?"

"Was that Lola's friend, Anna calling?"

"It was nobody."

"The way the Lord is blessing you, man, don't you think you can be a little more generous to Lola's best friend. She is worried, man."

"Lola made her swear she wouldn't tell you. We men on the team have told you things that you have never told anyone, because you are obligated to us. Not even our wives know everything we go through. It happens, man. Anna had an obligation to Lola. Remember, she almost died by this same man. Please just give her a break."

"I know you're right, but I don't feel like talking to no one right now. Can you maybe call her?"

Before Nick could make the call, the men looked down the hall and couldn't believe their eyes.

"Would you look at that?" Gabe said, laughing. All their wives came to be with them to give Lola and Hunter support.

"How is she?" Nick's wife asked.

"She is going to be okay. She will make a full recovery."

Gabe looked at Hunter and smiled. "Should we tell them?"

"Tell us what?" Peggy asked.

Taking a deep breath…smiling, Hunter told them he and Lola were having twins.

An hour later, the nurse came and told Hunter he could see Lola, but only him. Lola needed her rest.

"You go on and be with your woman, man," Gabe said, "we will meet at the safe house later."

Hunter walked in the room slowly.

"Hi," Lola said, smiling weakly.

"Hi," Hunter answered, kissing her on the cheek.

"Hunter, I am so sorry for leading you on that night," she said weakly.

"Shush, baby. You don't have to apologize. I'm glad you did."

"You are?" She asked weakly.

"Yes. I wanted to make love to you long before that night, but I wanted our relationship to be solid. I love you, Lola. I loved you when I first heard your voice. I always will."

"I'm pregnant, Hunter. I didn't mean to…" 'A tear rolled down her cheek.

"I was not trying to trap you into marriage. I was leaving because it would hurt too badly if I told you I was pregnant and you didn't want me and the baby."

He raised up and kissed her on the lips.

"I am glad you're pregnant. My little babies. My precious, precious little babies. Oh, Lola, I am so happy. I'm going to be a dad."

"Did you say babies, Hunter?'"

"Yes, baby, I did."

"The doctor didn't tell me. He did say it was something you wanted to tell me. Is it about the babies?"

"Yes." Hunter gently rubbed her stomach as a tear left his eyelid.

"Hunter?"

"Yes, baby."

"You're not mad? I mean there are two babies now. I didn't mean to burden you with one, now there's two."

"No, Lola. I am not mad. I am so thankful that you and the babies are alright. I have been thanking God for giving me my family to love."

He raised her hand and kissed it.

"Now, I need you to stop worrying and get better. I think our babies need a mother and a father that are living under the same roof."

Lola stared at Hunter with love and awe.

Could this be real, she thought in amazement.

Could this wonderful man want me and the babies? Oh, dear, God, she cried inside.

"What do you mean? Living under the same roof?"

"I mean, sweetheart. My intentions were always true where you are concerned. I love you, baby. I love my babies you are carrying. What I mean, Lola…"

Hunter made sure he had her full attention before he spoke again.

Sitting on the side of the bed, he held her hand and gazed into her beautiful eyes and said, "Lola, baby, will you marry me. I promise to take care of you and our babies…no matter how many you choose to give me."

A steady stream of tears were flowing down her cheeks. "Yes. Yes, I will marry you. Oh, Hunter," she sighed happily.

"Me and these babies love you so much."

She slowly reached for him. He leaned down so she could hold him. Her arms gently wrapped around him as their hearts beat as one.

"I know you do, baby."

"Hunter?"

"Yes?"

"You said, and I quote, 'no matter how many you choose to give me.', end quote. I thought you did the giving."

She could feel him smiling as she held him close.

"I guess I did, didn't I?"

"Yes you did."

"I think we are going to have a long hard talk about me giving you precious babies."

"Such as?" She asked, smiling tiredly.

"What it takes for me to give you those precious babies…when we have a house full, do we stop…"

Lola didn't let him get any further. Turning his head to her she proceeded to kiss him. "You mean stop doing that?"

"The question was hypothetical, baby. I will never be able to stop doing that…and more…much, much more."

"Whew!" she exclaimed, tiredly. "You had me scared there for a few seconds."

Hunter looked at Lola with love drenched eyes and asked why.

"Why? Well, love of my life. It will take a lifetime and beyond before I get enough of what you gave me the night we were together."

Hunter gently eased her down and stood up.

"Try not to talk like that again until we can do something about it. I know you are tired. I can see it in your eyes. It is time for you and my babies to get some rest."

"I will have a talk with your mother and father about us getting married when I can. Is that alright with you?"

"Yes," she said, lovingly.

He leaned down and kissed her before turning to leave. At the door she called his name.

"Yes?"

"Did you find out who paid you all that money to protect me?"

"Yes. We did. My team is very good at what they do. But I don't want to talk about it right now. You need your strength for you and the babies."

"Hunter?"

"Yes, sweetheart?"

"I know you are a very busy man, but do you think you can stay with me for a while? A little while. I feel so lonely when you are not around."

He slowly walked back to the bed, laid next to her, gently pulled her into his arms and said lovingly, "I am not going anywhere."

"Thank you."

Feeling the strength of this man whom she loved with all her heart, she whispered before she slept, "I love you, Hunter. I love you so much."

"I love you too, baby."

He lovingly massaged her hair and scalp and held her until she closed her eyes.

Hunter made sure Lola was sound asleep before he left the room.

"Nick, before you let Anna and Sam leave the safe house, make sure that Frank acted alone. I don't know what it is, but I am not at peace with Frank being out of the picture."

"Do you think he had a partner?"

"I don't know. I should be on top of the world that Lola is safe, and that Frank can't hurt her, but I don't feel safe. Something still seems to be missing."

"You think it may be because you love her so deeply and you just want to protect her and the babies?"

"I don't know, Nick. It is just a gut feeling I have. Of course, I love Lola and the babies deeply, but I have been doing this job too long. I could be tired, but I don't think so."

"Please keep checking into Frank's background. Remember he and Lola grew up together, yet and still, she didn't have any recollection of him when Frank was dating Anna."

"We're on it, boss."

Throwing in a little humor, Nick said, "I knew you liked Anna just a little bit. You don't want them to leave the safe house until you are sure it is safe."

"Nick, Anna was very careless with Lola at the safe house, and I don't particularly like her that much. But she is Lola's best friend and I know I am going to have to like her somewhat because it will make Lola happy."

"Anna, hi. How is the baby?" Lola asked, days later as she tried sitting up in bed.

Anna rushed to help her. Leaning down, Anna gave Lola a kiss on the cheek before sitting next to her.

"I'm doing okay. The baby is doing very well. He is only two and a half weeks old and, Lola, he is getting so big."

"Oh, wow! I can't wait to see him. How is Sam? I know he is over the moon with excitement."

"He is. He is taking care of Sammy. That's what we decided to name him. Sam wanted him to be a junior."

Lola smiled and Anna stared down at her hands in her lap.

"I would have come to see you sooner, but Hunter forbade me to come. Lola, I am so sorry. I thought I was doing the right thing by not telling Hunter you had left the safe house."

"Now Anna, you stop this right now. I begged you not to tell Hunter that I left. I thought he hated me. You did do the right thing. Your allegiance was to me. I was your friend, not Hunter."

"I know, but…"

"No buts, Anna. God blessed us all to get through this and we are all safe and that is what matters. Hunter will come around. Of course I did not know he loves me as much as he does. He is very happy about the twins."

Anna stared at Lola, surprise written on her face.

"You didn't know? No one told you about me having twins?"

"I told you, Hunter does not talk to me at all and the guys who work for him I don't know that well. Nick is okay, but his allegiance is to Hunter."

Putting her hands to her face in excitement, Anna squealed, "Oh, my Lola…twins. I am so happy for you. Congratulations."

Anna jumped from her chair and hugged Lola, her eyes tearing up.

"How long will you be in the hospital?"

"Maybe another week. Frank's knife cut left a nice size gash on my leg, but it is healing nicely. I won't be able to do a lot of walking, but I am thankful to be alive."

"And here I was thinking Frank had a hankering for me, but it was you he wanted all along. Talk about being blindsided."

"I know right. I'm just so happy that everything has turned out for the best for us all."

"Can you believe I actually slept with that psycho?" Anna said.

"Almost lost my friends because of that snake in the grass."

"Now, that…my friend, you really need to try and erase from your memory. You have Sam and the baby. A family. Build on that and trust God for the rest."

"I know you're right," Anna sighed. On a lighter note, Anna said, smiling.

"Sam and I are getting married, but we want to wait until you are out of the hospital."

"All this celebration and I'm stuck in this hospital. And I can't have any wine."

"After the babies are born, there will be plenty of time to celebrate."

Anna paused, looked at Lola cheekily and said, "You know, Hunter is not such a bad guy after all. I was wrong for thinking all on-line dates are Psychos from hell. I was very careless with Frank and almost paid the price with my life. And, although Hunter doesn't talk to me, I know he loves you."

"Thank you, Anna. Hunter is not bad at all. He is one of the good guys. I'm just so happy that he loves me and the twins. Hunter likes you, he is still a little pissed that you did not tell him I had left. But he will come around."

"At the safe house when I finally told him you had left and he found out that you were pregnant, I never want to see that look on his face again. It's as if he literally crumbled in front of us. Then he got so mad he could barely contain his rage. I am so glad that Sam was there or he might have shaken me to near death to get the truth from me about where you had gone."

"Was it really that bad?" Lola asked.

"Yes, Lola. It really was that bad. He promised to take the baby if I didn't tell him where you were. I knew at that time how much he truly loved you. Please don't ever ask me to lie for you again, especially to Hunter."

"I won't."

"Well, I better be going. I don't want to leave little Sammy too long with Sam and I know Hunter probably got one of his men spying to see how long I'm staying. Or if I am tiring you out," Anna said on a happy note, getting up to hug Lola.

"Take care of yourself and the twins. I love you, Lola."

"I love you too. Bye for now."

Sliding down in the bed after Anna left, Lola began to shiver uncontrollable, but didn't know why.

"Dear God, what is wrong with me? I can't stop shivering," she whispered, feeling impending doom.

She reached for her phone on the nightstand to call Hunter.

"Lola, baby is everything okay?"

"Yes, I'm alright…now. Is everything alright with you?" She asked, trying to keep the fear from her voice.

"Yeah. We had to tie up some loose ends with other cases we're working on, but overall everything is going good here. I was coming by later this evening and sit with you…keep you company, but if…"

"Oh, Hunter. I was hoping you would come by. I miss you."

"Okay, baby. I'll see you soon. Love you, baby."

"I love you too, sweetheart."

Before he could hang-up, she called his name again.

"I'm still here. Did you need me to bring you something when I come?"

Not bothering to answer his question, she asked one of her own.

"Hunter, did Frank die when your man shot him?"

"Yes. He died instantly. He can't hurt you, baby."

"Okay," she said, not sounding so sure.

"I tell you what, I'll wrap things up and come over now. Will that make you feel better?"

"Yes. Thank you," she said, feeling better now that Hunter was coming. She swiped her phone off.

"Hello?"

Lola jumped.

Where did this man come from standing over her, her mind thought?

Who is he?

"Excuse me, but I think you have the wrong room," she said hesitantly.

"Are you Ms. Wells?"

"I said you need to leave. I don't know you and I want you to leave. Right now!"

8

Instead of leaving, the man only stared at Lola the more, giving her the creeps. He needed to leave.

"I asked you to leave," she said, voice getting louder. Fear was beginning to grip her. She instantly thought about her babies. One crazy psycho had already tried to kill them. Reaching for the call button, he told her there was no need to do that, he just wanted to know if her name was Ms. Lola Wells.

"Help!" she called out. "Help!" she cried the louder.

"You don't have to do that," he said, walking away swiftly.

Seconds later. "Ms. Wells, is there a problem," the nurse asked when she rushed into the room.

"There was a man in my room asking me questions," Lola said fearfully. "Didn't you see him? He was just in here."

"A lot of people walk past our station, Ms. Wells. I am sorry. He could have walked past us and we would not have paid much attention to him. A lot of visitors are coming and going. Did he hurt you in any way?"

"No! He just kept asking about my name, and he scared me." The nurse came and checked her vitals.

"Okay, Ms. Wells. We will alert security. But, in the meantime, I'm going to need you to calm down. Your pressure is rising and that is not good for you or the babies."

Lola tried to relax, but to no avail. *That man should not have been in my room,* she thought. *Who is he?*

The nurses had not been apprised of her situation so they wouldn't know to watch more closely the people that came on the floors.

Relaxing her head on the pillow, she told the nurse she would try and relax. After a mild sedative she was able to doze off talking to her babies as she caressed her stomach.

"Daddy will be here soon."

She woke up with Hunter staring at her.

"Hunter," she said, trying to sit up in bed, but the pain in her leg caused her to wince.

Hunter quickly stood and helped her to sit up.

"Wait, baby. Let me help you."

"Thank you," she said, smiling.

"That's better?"

"Yes."

"You sounded worried about something on the phone. Are you in a lot of pain? Are the babies okay?"

Hunter was holding her hand comfortingly and it made her feel safe, but she had to tell him about the man and the uneasy feeling and the nervous shaking.

"We are fine, but Hunter, something happened earlier that scared me."

"What happened?" The hairs on the back of his neck was tingling. *Dear God, what now?* He thought.

"Well, it might not be nothing, but…"

"Lola, baby. Let me be the judge of that. What happened?"

"When I finished talking with you on the phone, I was swiping my phone off when a man said hello. I looked up and he was here. I mean here, in my room. He scared me so badly I asked him to leave immediately. He kept asking me if my name was Lola Wells."

"You say you have never seen this man before?"

"No. Never. Hunter, what is going on? I thought after Frank's death, everything would be okay."

"Can you remember what he looked like? Tall? Short? Bald? Mustache?"

"I know this might sound crazy, but he had a strong resemblance to Frank, but when Frank and I played together when we were young, there were just the two of us. There were no other children on the block."

"How do you feel?"

"I'm still a little shaky, but I am okay now that you're here."

"I am signing you out of the hospital and taking you home with me. My doctor is on standby and he is good. Is that okay with you?"

"Yes," she said, feeling better already. "You sure it's okay for me to stay with you? I don't want to get in the way."

"I am sure," he said, standing. "No worries, I live alone."

"Oh, I almost forgot. Your secretary, Pam, called to check on you."

"She is the best. How is she doing?"

"She is doing great. Holding the fort down at the office until you get back. She asked if she could come see you. I told her I would check with you and let her know."

An hour later Hunter helped Lola to his SUV, missing the figure in the shadows watching them.

"Is this your home?" Lola asked, scanning the grounds surrounding the mansion-like house forty minutes later.

"No. I usually live here when I have work in Atlanta."

"You must have some very rich and generous friends," Lola said in awe. "This house is beautiful. I love it."

Hunter looked straight ahead, said nothing, and just smiled.

Inside Lola looked around.

"Hunter, are you sure the owners don't mind me staying here with you. I mean, they might not mind you staying here, but maybe I better stay at the safe house with Anna for a while."

Hunter walked up to Lola and softly touched her face. "Come on."

"Where are we going? Hunter, you didn't answer me. Hunter?" Lola said, uneasily.

Taking her hand, he gently led her to a bedroom, but she pulled back before going inside.

"Lola. I am not going to hurt you. I only want you to lie down and relax while we talk."

Slowly she walked into the bedroom and sat on the side of the bed.

"You can leave now. I don't have anything to wear. I think this was a bad idea."

Hunter walked over to the drawer and pulled out some night clothes.

"Here's two night shirts. Either one will do. They are both below the knee and you will be covered."

Sitting back down on the bed beside her, he humorously said, "You do know I have seen you with no clothes on."

"I know, but this is different."

When he hesitated, before he could say more, she spoke.

"Please, Hunter. I kinda messed that up for us. I let my feelings get the best of me."

Hunter massaged her stomach gently and asked her, "Can you really say you messed that night up for us? There is a miracle growing in here," he said, pressing her stomach a little stronger, feeling the baby bump.

"Are you truly happy I am pregnant?"

"Yes. As God is my witness. I wouldn't change a thing. Well, I would change maybe one thing."

"You want the twins and not me?"

"What? No. What we shared that night went way beyond the physical. Baby you touched my soul. I can still feel a part of you with me."

He kissed her on the forehead.

"The only thing I would change is us being married. What we shared as man and woman that night was not a cheap romp in the hay. It was real. I still feel it."

"Goodness, Hunter," she said emotionally, "no wonder I want you all the time. You are a man above men. You are strong. Loving. Intelligent. A protector, and the best lover in the universe. I am trying to fight my need for, but like that night, it is very hard."

Hunter pulled her to him and held her close.

"Hunter?"

"Yes," he whispered.

He followed her eyes staring below his waist. Raising her eyes to his, he was totally surprised at the passion her eyes were exuding. Her question surprised him even more when she asked in a sultry voice, "Did I cause that?"

"Yes, baby you did. You can't talk like that and think I won't be affected. My love for you runs just as deeply as your love for me."

"I can fix that for you if you want me too," she sighed.

"I want you to fix it so badly cause, baby I am aching all over."

Holding her closer he said matter of factly, "But I am not going to, not right now."

"But, I don't mind," she whispered, lovingly.

"Lola, baby. I am so blessed to have a woman that is hotter than lava from a volcano, who knows how to please her man, but for now you are going to rest that leg and take care of our babies." He held her away from him, smiling lovingly at her.

"You asked me earlier to leave and that is what I am going to do. Now do you promise to lie down and get some rest? We will talk later."

"Yes. I promise." At the door he heard her gasp in pain. He immediately rushed back to her side.

Slowly and gently he eased her clothes off and put on one of the shirts.

"Lie down and I will put a pillow under your leg."

"Feel better?"

"Yes. Thank you."

Walking to the dresser, he pulled out a brush and comb. "Hunter, what are you doing now?" She wailed softly.

Don't you know I am about to jump your bones, she thought madly.

"Well, my love. I am going to brush and comb your hair. If you had taken just one look in the mirror at that beautiful, gorgeous hair you always keep in place you would have ran and hid."

"Oh," she said, bottom lip beginning to tremble.

"I know I look bad, but you could have saved me some dignity and said nothing."

Hunter smiled and kept walking to the bed.

"Honey, you did ask me what I was doing."

"Go away, Hunter. Don't you dare touch my hair."

Sitting on the side of the bed, he made a deep dent in the mattress causing her to sway towards him.

He used the opportunity to lay her head on his shoulder and began brushing her hair.

Oh this has got to be heaven on earth, she thought as the brush massaged her scalp.

Yet and still, she thought madly, *he had no right telling her how bad I look.*

Raising her head felt like being delivered straight to hell, but she did it anyway.

"Leave my room, Hunter," she said weakly.

"I can brush my own hair."

"I was trying to be a little humorous because I know you had a fright earlier," he explained. "My bad. I am sorry. I will leave you alone and come check on you later. Is that what you want?"

"No, Hunter. That is not what I want."

"I see I really angered you," he said, getting up from the bed. "I will be back later. Okay, baby?"

"No, Hunter. That is not okay," she wailed miserably.

"Lola, baby. You have to tell me what you want. I have not been in love at this magnitude before. You are pregnant with my babies and I want to be here for you, but I seem to be doing it all wrong."

"Hunter, please sit back down on the bed."

He sat down and waited, keeping his mouth totally shut.

Lola laid her head on his chest and softly wept.

"What is it, baby? I am here. Talk to me. I will never hurt you…at least not knowingly."

"Hold me, Hunter," she sighed. He held her silently, thinking it better not to say anything.

"Oh, sweetheart," she sighed again, lovingly.

"Please brush my hair. It felt like heaven when you did it before."

"Well, baby why did…" Hunter started and quickly stopped, realizing her need for him and her pregnant hormones were running rampant in her body. He continued brushing her hair as she lay on him.

Hunter was waiting for her to go to sleep so he could run from temptation. Her soft pliable body was working havoc on his body. He felt her breasts as they worked as one with her breathing, heating his chest each time they went up and down.

"Hunter?" She whispered, holding him tighter.

Taking a deep breath before he answered, "Yes?"

"I love you. Oh how I love you," she moaned, holding him even closer.

Oh, dear, God. Please help, he prayed. He could feel the heat from her body.

"I love you, too, baby. Your hair is beautiful again, so I am going to lie you down so you can get some rest."

"Hunter?"

Please don't ask, he thought. *Please don't ask me to make love to you. Not tonight, Lola. Please*, he begged silently.

"Yes, baby?"

"Will you please sleep with me tonight?"

"I can't, baby."

She was about to pull away, but he held her close. Refusing to leave her mad at him.

"Relax, sweetheart. Let me explain why I said what I said."

Hunter began to explain when he felt her body relax against him.

"Lola, baby I fell in love with you when I heard your voice. When I saw your picture, I was hooked. The night we made love was the best night of my life. I haven't felt anything that good in all of my life. I have wanted you every day since that night, but I refuse to continue to make love to you and not make you an honest woman. I want you so bad right now, my toes are aching. I feel like my eyes are about to burst from my face. And you don't want to know about the other parts of my body."

He gently eased her from his shoulder and stared her in her eyes. "Lola, baby. Your leg is healing. You are caring my babies and you have been traumatized and you need your rest. Sweetheart, I would be less than a man if I took advantage of you now. I refuse to. I can't sweetheart. Please don't hate me."

"I don't hate you, sweetheart," she whispered, easing her lips to his.

"Lola," Hunter said between kisses, not wanting to hurt her feelings. "Baby, we need to stop. Please, sweetheart."

Putting her lips to his ear, matter of factly, she spoke.

"I know I need to rest. But I also know I need this from you. Thank you for thinking of me and the babies, but sweetheart, you are going to have to give me some part of you or I will not be able to get any rest."

Hunter held her away from him, staring into her beautiful brown eyes lowering his head to give her a goodnight kiss.

When his body froze, Lola opened her eyes to see what had stopped Hunter from kissing her. Hunter quickly stepped away from the bed.

"Hunter? Baby, what is it?"

"Sshh, baby. Please be quiet."

Hunter turned to Lola.

"Stay in this room. Do not come out. Do you understand?"

The look in his eyes said it all. He was not only cautious, she saw fear in his eyes.

She knew it was not fear for him, but for her. To reassure him, she quickly said, "Yes. I understand."

Not turning on any lights, he walked to the window and through a small opening, he scanned the front yard.

Frustrated, he saw nothing. No One.

"What is going on?" he whispered. "I know Frank is dead," he whispered. "He couldn't have worked alone."

He quickly walked back to Lola.

At the door, he saw her with her knees to her chest, she was rocking back and forth. The sight smote his heart.

Sitting on the bed when he sat down, she was about to scream.

Pulling her into his arms, he held her safely. She was trembling like a leaf on a tree in a storm.

"It's me, baby. I'm here."

He held her away from him to get her attention.

"Lola. Listen to me, baby. I am not going to let anything or no one harm you. I will give my life first if it means it will keep you and my babies safe."

"Okay, baby?" He prodded.

"Okay. But, Hunter, don't you know if something were to happen to you, I would have a hard time wanting to live. Goodness, Hunter. Don't you know how much I love you and these babies?"

"Lola. Sweetheart. I need to know if something were to happen to me, you have to have and raise our babies."

Lola eased from Hunter's arms, slowly, very slowly she began to walk to the bathroom.

"Lola. You don't need to be walking a lot on your leg." Although, it hurt, she turned to him and with determination, said,

"Hunter, God saw fit to send me one of the best men on this planet. He even saw fit to give us two little babies and I will be damned if I let someone come along and take you and these babies away from me. I don't know what is going on or who is out to hurt me, but I will never be scared out of my wits again like I was tonight."

She held out her hand to Hunter. They walked to the bathroom together.

"I want you so bad, Hunter David Nichols, I am now shaking from my need for you and not fright, but I do understand what you were saying earlier. Would it be too hard on you if you helped me shower?"

"Too hard on me in what way?" He asked. *This woman has got to know what she is doing to me,* he thought.

She stared down below his waist, afraid to look up to see the look in his eyes. She knew she was playing with fire, but she wanted to get burned so badly by this man she was beyond caring.

"Well, I know you are a man and you will see me with nothing on and…" she was finding it difficult to go on. Now she was feeling embarrassed and acting like a whorish woman.

Not trying to hide what he knew she saw, he said, "No. It's not too hard on me."

Liar, liar, pants on fire, his thoughts battled in his mind. Instead of arguing with his mind he turned on the shower and when it was warm enough, helped her into the shower.

"Aren't you coming in?" She asked.

Hunter breathed out a breath he did not know he was holding until then. He did not have to look down to know he was very aroused and showing like crazy. When he looked at Lola, her eyes were glued to the lower part of his body.

"I think I will just sit over there on the stool until you finish your shower."

"If I stand near the edge, will you wash my back?"

"I don't think you should be worrying about your back. Just rinse off and I can help you out of the shower."

Lola wanted Hunter with a hunger she had never experienced before. When he stopped at the side of the shower to wash her back, she did not turn for him to wash her back. Instead, she quickly unzipped his pants and fastened onto the object of her desire. It happened so fast, Hunter could do nothing but stare at her.

"Why, Hunter, what is this?" She asked, staring below his waist as she softly caressed him. Lola knew she was wrong, but she didn't care.

I love this man with all my heart and I am carrying his babies and I am so horny, she thought, *I am about to lose my mind.*

"You minx. You know exactly what that is and you better be good or suffer the consequences."

"What are the consequences, Hunter?" She asked in a sultry voice stepping from the shower.

"Lola, baby, please be careful," he said, helping her to keep her balance.

Paying him no heed, of their own volition, her hands began to massage him.

"Oh, baby don't," Hunter sighed, barely able to stand.

"Oh, baby, yes," she moaned, gripping him tighter, refusing to let him go.

"The babies, Lola. You need your strength," Hunter tried again, his body about to explode with burning desire. Hunter tried to move her hand from his joystick, but she held on to him fiercely without hurting him.

"I am sorry, Hunter, but I can't let you go, baby. I love you too much. I need you too badly."

When she pulled him down and began kissing on him, Hunter hollered out insanely. Before he lost all his senses, he carried her to the bed.

"Lola, baby," he sighed on the bed. "I love you. So much."

"Show me, Hunter. Please. Just don't hate me like you did before."

"I didn't hate you," he sighed. "I was afraid of my feelings. I will explain later. Okay, baby?"

"Okay. You showed me so good the last time, that's how I got these babies."

Hunter realized he was losing it again, but couldn't help himself.

Lola cried out in the throes of passion so passionately, he asked if he had hurt her.

"No," she sighed wantonly. "I love you, Hunter," she continued to sigh, barely able to take what he was doing to her. "I need you, Hunter. I need you."

As the force of their love continued to meet head on, Hunter thought he was losing his mind. Total sensual oblivion gripped their bodies when Hunter guttural sounds tore at her love for him. Holding him closer, her grip held him so tight, his body exploded. Trembling, Hunter used his arms to hold his weight off her, but he could not move. He never wanted to move. He was where he wanted to be.

"Hold me, Hunter," she whispered.

"I'm too heavy, baby," he whispered, too weak to talk loudly.

"Please, baby," she whispered. "Hold me and never let me go."

Thinking of the babies and her fragile state, he only held her for a few seconds. Raising himself from her, she stopped him.

9

"Don't move, Hunter," she moaned. "Not now. Please not now. Share your strength with me, sweetheart."

Wanting to please her, he lay on her for a few seconds more. His mind stayed on the babies and her sore leg. He was their protector and he always wanted to be there for them. He was about to get up when she started moving beneath him. He immediately began to grow.

"Oh, baby," he sighed, feeling his passion begin to stir for her. "Oh, Lola, baby please," he sighed.

"Hunter?"

"Yes?"

"Will you hate me for wanting you again," she asked as she continued to move beneath him.

"I could never hate you, baby. How could I hate you when I love you so much? I want you so badly my body is burning out of control? I just don't want you to overdo it."

The more she moved her body, the more she burned him. Her passion was infiltrating his body. What she did next with her body, Hunter groaned in total submission. His mumbled words of love made no sense to his ears, but he knew his beloved understood.

She had worn herself out from making love so many times. Hunter had bathed her in bed to keep her from exerting herself. But when she looked at him and saw how gentle he was being with her. How tender and lovingly he bathed her, only threw her body into a whirlwind of passionate need again.

I never thought I could be this hungry and exude this much passion for a man, but with Hunter my body stays on fire, she thought.

Her body was filled with so much raw passion and sensual hunger, she had thrown caution to the wind, pulled Hunter to the bed and had her way with him.

Her passionate fury on his body released his animal hunger he had been holding back from her. Hunter met Lola's passion so deeply she cried out from feelings so devastatingly out of this world, her body froze in time.

She could only stare from love drenched eyes at the wonderful man whom she loved with all her heart. Pulling her lower body to his, his powerful force sent sensual shock waves through her body that held her captive in his grasp.

"Oh, Hunter," she cried from her soul.

"Oh, baby," she sighed, passionately.

"I love you," she moaned, realizing she had unleashed a force so powerful in him, she was just going to have to enjoy the ride. There was no stopping him from the strength he was exuding.

"I've got too baby," he groaned. "I can't stop, sweetheart."

"If you stop now, baby," she sighed, "I will die. You can't stop. I love you."

"Oh," he cried, seconds later.

"Lola. Baby," he groaned with barely controlled emotions as he exploded causing fireworks to go off in all directions in his body.

When he rolled from her later, he pulled her to his chest. Running his hand through her hair, he realized that it was not the babies that had drawn them together, but it had been this total bonding that had tied them together. He knew beyond the shadow of a doubt that what they just shared had bonded them together for the rest of their lives.

"Thank you."

"For what?" He asked.

"For loving me. I needed that from you so badly and you did not disappoint."

"You are welcome, baby," he said. Smiling, he said humorously, "Of course, my little minx, I think it was you who had your way with me. Baby, you know you wore me out?"

Smiling back, she reached up and kissed him and said, "Sweetheart, you woke me up from my virginity. You showed me a whole new world that entire night. You awakened needs in me that only you can satisfy. That morning you left angry and hurt, but you also left me totally in love with you…with feelings I had never felt before. Tonight, I needed to feel all your strength. I know you had been taking it easy with me because of the babies and my leg, but I needed you, sweetheart."

"Did I give you what you needed? Did you get satisfied?"

"Oh, yes. With a capital S." She leaned in closer. "I love you, Hunter."

"I know you do, baby. I love you too." Lying on his chest, she felt it shaking with laughter.

"What?" She asked.

"You have a very healthy appetite for loving. Baby, you can go on and on and on. The bunny rabbit ain't got nothing on you."

"It is all your fault. You do know that don't you?"

"Me?" He asked, faking innocence. "Why Lola Wells, you ravished me."

"Should I apologize?" She asked.

"No way," he said. "Never apologize for needing me. I like that fire in you. And I like to feel needed. You did kinda surprise me with your passion. You don't hold back and I love that about you. You really don't tire easily."

"Stop making it so good. Maybe I wouldn't want it so much. Now you have marked me for life."

"Good. Cause I don't want another man touching you. Period."

To his surprise, she reached down and held his joystick in her hand. Breathing a long sigh of contentment, she was alright with the world.

"Hunter?"

"Yes, baby?"

"Is this all mine?"

Hunter did a little chuckle. "Are we a little jealous?"

"I am a lot jealous. I don't want no other woman feeling what you make me feel."

"Yes, baby," he said, holding her closer. "It is all yours for as long as you want it."

"I guess forever and fifty years ought to be enough time to call it my own. I love you, Hunter."

"I know you do, sweetheart. I love you too. Very much."

"How is your leg? Does it hurt at all?"

"What leg?" She asked.

"Damn, baby. Was it really that good to you? I thought your leg would be a little sore…you know…when the sexy feelings wore off."

"Who said they wore off?" She asked, holding him tighter in her hand.

"It would appear your sexiness hasn't worn off either," she whispered.

"As long as you're doing what you're doing it's not going to wear off any time soon."

"Which is a shame," she yawned. "If you had not worn me out, I would give you a run for your money with this body. But, to answer your question, yes, my leg feels much better."

"Good. Now, please get some rest, and behave."

"Okay, baby."

When she was asleep, he eased from the bed. He couldn't sleep. Their loving had been so out of this world good it should have knocked him out cold, but he was feeling very uneasy again. *God, I love this woman and my babies now more than ever,* he thought. *We truly bonded tonight.*

But someone is out there, and Hunter didn't think they were far away, who wanted to hurt Lola. Frank had to have had a partner.

Not wanting to scare Lola any more than she had been, he did not tell her, but he could have sworn someone was trying to get in downstairs. He knew they could never get in the doors or the windows. The locks were second to none, but he had been careless about the alarm system and not turned it on. *I didn't think no one would follow me here*, he thought.

"Who wants my baby this badly and why," he whispered.

He didn't know how Lola was going to take it, but she had to go into hiding again at the safe-house. He knew they couldn't follow them there.

Two weeks later at the safe house

"Lola it is so good to see you," Pam said, hugging Lola.

"Same here. Sit down and tell me what's been going on since I left. It seems so long ago. Better still, do I even have a job?"

"Of course, you do. You lost a few of your clients, but most of them remained faithful. I just miss you so much. When you told me they got the guy that was stalking you, I thought everything was over."

"Girl, we did too. But, Hunter seems to believe he had a partner working with him. Sometimes an eerie feeling comes over me and I get the chills and fear tries to rear its ugly head, but I am determined not to let it get me down."

"Ms. Lola, I am so sorry this is happening to you. Is there anything I can do?"

"Thank you, Pam, but you are doing enough already. By the way, are we making enough money for you to give yourself at least a ten percent raise?"

"To be honest, your wealth has definitely grown, but I am not worried about a raise. I just miss you and will be glad when you are back at work." Pam looked at Lola skeptically.

"Ms. Wells, you did say it was okay for me to give your financial report to Mr. Hunter so he can make sure no clients are trying to cheat you while you are out sick?"

"Yes. That is okay. I know you are good at what you do for me, but I just want a second pair of eyes..."

"You don't have to explain everything to me. All those numbers just go around in my head. One night my husband said I was talking numbers in my sleep."

"How is he doing?"

Blushing, Pam looked down before saying, "He is doing well."

"Say no more," Lola said, smiling on the verge of laughing. "Your face says it all. You know we have to hold on to the good guys."

"I know. You are so right."

There was a tap on the door.

"Am I interrupting you ladies?"

Pam took a look at Lola and knew she was a goner. Her love for this man was radiating from every fiber of her being.

"Actually, I was just leaving," Pam said, kissing Lola on the forehead. "Take care of my niece and nephew. Love you, girl."

"Love you more. Thanks again for holding down the fort."

"Bye, Mr. Hunter."

"Take care, Ms. Pam."

Hunter kissed Lola on the forehead. Lola knew he was there to talk seriously. Something was on his mind.

"Lola. Did you ever know your parents?"

What kind of question is that? She thought.

"What do you mean, Hunter? Of course, I know my parents."

"Baby. I don't quite know how to tell you this…"

Hunter appeared to be having a hard time telling her what he had to tell her.

"Hunter, please just spit it out. You're making me much more nervous by your actions."

"The man you believed to be your father is not your father."

For the first time, Lola thought she had caught Hunter in a lie. The man she loved dearly. With all her heart. *For God's sake,* she thought madly, *I am carrying his children.*

"How can you say that to me?" She said, trying to stand from her anger, but cried out from the pain when she turned the wrong way.

Hunter was by her side immediately. She tried pushing him away and cried out the more. Hunter picked her up and gently eased her back to the couch.

"Get away from me, Hunter. I don't like you too much right now. I mean, how could you say that? My dad raised me. He is good to me. My mother…" Hunter was not saying anything. He only stared at her with love.

"My mother. I mean my father. My mother never said anything. I mean my dad."

Lola couldn't go on. The love she saw in Hunter's eyes. The pain mixed with love. His body language. She realized he was not lying to her.

When he saw the first tear fall he quickly sat by her side, pulled her in his arms and whispered, "We are going to get through this, baby. Together. Trust me. There is so much more to tell you, and I am going to need you to be strong."

Picking her up he carried her to one of the bedrooms, laid her down and laid down next to her and wrapped her in his arms.

"Sweetheart, you picked a fine time to want to make love," she said, smiling.

"We are not going to make love, Lola. At least not yet. Baby, you have got to let your leg heal. I lost it before, but I can't go at you that hard again until we see the doctor. He is coming by later today to look at your leg. For now, I just want to hold you and give you support while I explain about your father."

"Has my entire life been a lie?" She asked in his arms.

"No, baby. Your dad. The man that raised you for all intents and purposes is your father. He loves you very much. He wanted to tell you, but your mother forbade him."

"But why?"

"Well, it would appear she wanted nothing to do with your biological father so she kept him away from you as well."

"But that is not telling me why she did what she did. Why keep my father away from me?"

"Mr. Hamm, that is his name, was Hawaiian and your mother was embarrassed when he walked out on her. She truly loved him, but when she became pregnant, he just up and left. Said he didn't want a family. Couldn't afford one. Left your mother devastated. Baby, she was going to abort you, but the man you know as your father stopped her, asked to marry her and the rest is history."

"Why was she going to abort me?"

"People had warned her about Mr. Hamm. Told her he only wanted her for her beauty and her body. I saw a picture of your mother and she is devastatingly beautiful. Even now. When I saw her picture I saw her beauty in you. Your mother didn't want to face the shame of people saying, 'I told you so,' but the day she was to abort you, she met your dad, Mr. Wells."

"He fell in love with her instantly."

"You mean he fell in love with her beauty," she said, sarcastically.

"It happens, baby. I fell in love with your voice. However, as much as I love you, I didn't truly bond with you until we made love. Something happens to me when I enter your body. I loved you from the time I met you. I even gave you two babies the first time we made love, but when we made love on that night at the house where I was staying, when you loved my body the way you did and unleashed a side of me I never knew I had, it was as if our souls bonded as one never to be two again."

He held her face with both hands. "Do you understand what I'm saying?"

"Yes. I felt it too…all over. My insides exploded, our love was so wonderful."

Damn, Hunter thought, he wanted her right now and all they were doing was talking about their love. But she needed to hear what he had to say.

"So, please, give your mother and both fathers a break. Emotions of the heart is no joke and are nothing to play with."

"So, are you saying that my real father paid for my protection?"

"Yes."

"But why, Hunter?"

"I mean, he left me and my mother and didn't want anything to do with us. Why is he coming back into my life? I love my father. He took care of mom and me. I want no part of Mr. Hamm. Not now."

"I understand, baby, but we have got to get to the bottom of this. Someone out there is still trying to hurt you, baby. And I think Mr. Hamm knows more and my team and I are going to find out."

Massaging her scalp and holding her close, he asked, "Will it be okay if I bring your mother and father here to see you? They have filed a missing person's report on you."

"I haven't been gone that long."

Hunter looked at her sideways.

"Sweetheart it has been months. They are very worried." He had a worried look on his face.

"What is it, Hunter?"

"I need to ask them some questions."

"Why?" She asked, looking worried.

"Something is not adding up, baby. Someone is lying and I need to know who…and why."

"Well, it has to be Mr. Hamm. He is the one who left momma and me. Maybe he hates the fact that I lived and momma lived a happy life with dad."

"Then, baby. Why would he pay half a million dollars to my firm to keep you safe?"

"Maybe he paid it to throw us off his evil deeds."

"If that is the case…that would mean that Frank and Mr. Hamm must have known each other."

"But, Frank is dead and if Mr. Hamm is truly in Hawaii, someone here is still after you. That is why I need to go to Hawaii and have a talk with Mr. Hamm."

"Hunter, please…"

"Lola, baby, you are going to have to let me do my job. I need to talk with the man. I believe he has answers to my questions. I am ready to put all this behind us and live our lives. You are getting bigger and bigger with the babies."

"I am ready for us to get married. Have a home. All the works of married life. But, we can't while someone is out there threatening to harm you. You just have to trust me on this one."

"I do trust you. I want the same things. I hate you having to leave me and the babies. I almost hate Mr. Hamm for messing up my life. I know it's him who wants to hurt me."

Holding her close, he continued to massage her hair and scalp. What he wasn't prepared for was her outburst.

"Hunter, will you please stop running your fingers through my hair? I can't stand it. I can't stand it, I tell you."

With a hurt look on his face, he immediately stopped massaging her hair and scalp and eased from the bed.

"I am sorry, Lola. I was trying to comfort you. I know this is a lot to take in, I meant no harm."

Lola saw the hurt look on Hunter's face and her heart smote her. *To hurt Hunter is to hurt me and the babies*, she thought, jumping from the bed straight into his chest she held him tightly.

"I'm sorry, baby," she said, kissing him unashamedly.

"My hormones are all over the place."

She would never know where she got the strength from to pop the buttons from his shirt, but she did.

"I know I hurt you, baby," she sighed, getting his pants loose and pushing them down.

"You touch me and I want you," she mumbled, reaching for him.

"In some way, shape and form, my parents have hurt me," she continued, pulling him to the floor and throwing her blouse over her head.

"But, Hunter, baby you have never hurt me. Maybe you will in the future, but never so far."

Lola kissed Hunter as if her life depended on it.

"The only way you can hurt me now is to deny me yourself," she moaned, covering his body with her own.

"Lola, baby we can't," he said between her kisses.

"Your leg, Lola. The babies," he said, trying to ease her from him without hurting her feelings. She read his thoughts. Leaning down, she captured his lower body and talked the language of old.

She is getting better and better with knowing how to please me, Hunter thought as he threw his head back and cried out ferociously.

Lola had him in her grip and wouldn't let go. Her fierce affectionate loving was driving him crazy.

"Lola, baby please don't take me there," he grunted, moving fiercely unable to control himself. She was the only woman who could take him deep within himself and find raw passions that were hard to come back from.

He tried one last time, knowing he was already too far gone. His love for her. The feelings she brought out in him only fanned the flames of passion to a wildfire in his body.

"Baby, please," he sighed, body burning with no end in sight.

Staring at Lola from love drenched eyes, he knew she was too far gone to stop. She needed this as much as he wanted it. His body was the fiddle and she was strumming it to perfection.

"Hunter, you drive me crazy. You hear me? Crazy," she sighed going wild on his body. She couldn't get enough of this man.

"I used to be so in control of my feelings…until you came along. I never thought…"

"I never thought…Oh, Hunter," she wailed in passion. Lola stopped talking. What she felt for the man, she had to show him. Words could not convey her feelings.

"I know what you are trying to say, my sweet baby," he whispered shakily, caught in her web of unknown passions. The more Hunter hollered out, the more she set him aflame.

"Lola," he almost screamed before rolling her to her back.

At her entrance, Lola thought she would float away. Meeting together was a collision of the best kind. It was almost too wonderful, she thought, bearing her soul to Hunter. Their words had turned gibberish. No words were needed. Their bodies spoke for them. He caused her body to spasm like nothing she had felt before.

Wanting to please him like never before, the guttural sounds coming from his throat caused her to grip him so tight, the little control Hunter was holding on to snapped. His movements became so powerful, Lola thought he would send her through the floor. She loved it as she gripped him even tighter.

"Oh. Oh," he shouted softly, exploding so powerfully, he hollered out erratically. Seconds later, he wrapped her in his arms never wanting to let her go.

"Lola, baby," he sighed, resting his head on her shoulder. Remembering they were on the floor, he gently lifted her and eased her on the bed, but did not lie with her. Instead, he went and ran her bath water, thanking God the carpet on the floor was inches thick.

Running her bath water, Hunter lifted his eyes above. "Lord, I don't know what I did to deserve this wonderful woman and my two little ones, but please help get us through this so we can live as a family."

10

A week later, Hunter told Lola that her parents were coming to see her at the safe house.

"Do you feel up to seeing them?"

"Yes. I love my parents. My father stood by me when my biological dad left us. I never want to see Mr. Hamm."

"Are you sure? You have not heard his side of the story."

"Yes. I am sure," she said. "Why would I? He means nothing to me."

Sitting down beside her on the couch, he held her hand. "Lola, baby. I am going to Hawaii to have a talk with Mr. Hamm."

"Do you have to? Why can't we just leave things the way they are? I have mom and dad here with me. I don't need that man in my or my babies' lives."

"Honey, something still is not adding up. Don't you want the truth?"

"Well, yes. I do want the truth…" She couldn't go on.

"Are you afraid of the truth?"

Lola stared at Hunter and realized that the only truth was the love she saw in Hunter's eyes as he watched her reactions. A man that wanted to protect her and their babies with his life if he had to.

"Will you be by my side no matter how this turns out? No matter what happens or what we find out?"

"Yes. I will be here by your side no matter what. I want to protect you in every way that I can, but some things might come out before all this is over that could hurt you very badly."

"No, Hunter. I am not afraid of the truth. Whatever it is," she whispered softly as she leaned on his shoulder.

"When are you leaving?"

"Tomorrow morning. Nick will bring your parents by around noon tomorrow."

"Okay. Hunter, please be careful. I can bear a lot of things, but…" He stopped her before she finished.

"I will be careful, baby." He kissed her on the forehead. "What I need you to do is take care of my babies and their mom whom I love dearly."

He held her face in his hands softly.

"Will you do that for me?"

She turned her face and kissed his hand.

"Yes," she said lovingly.

"Some of my guys will be here. You won't see them but they will be around."

He gave her a small device and told her to press it if she needed anything or felt danger to her or her parents. All the guys will be able to hear that sound and come to you."

Hunter gently held her away from him.

"Will you do me a favor?" He asked her.

"Yes. You know I will."

"Could you not let your parents know about the device I gave you? I don't want no one knowing about it. Not yet, anyway."

"Okay." He saw the questions in her eyes, but he didn't know who to trust for now.

"Hopefully, I will have more to tell you when I get back from Hawaii."

"Please be careful," she told him, holding him tightly. He wrapped her in his arms and held her for seconds.

"I will. Take care of our babies." Kissing her intimately, he let her go and saw the tears on her cheeks.

"It's alright, baby. I'll be back in a few days."

"You better. Hunter, you better. We, me and the babies love you something fierce."

"I know, sweetheart." A final kiss, he was gone.

The next morning, Lola was excited. She had not seen her parents in a year. Looking around the room, it was huge and it was comfortable, but where would her parents sleep? She had forgotten to ask Hunter. The thought of her man, she smiled. He had called her to let her know he had made it safe and that he loved her.

Caressing her stomach, she was happy. She wanted to share her happiness with her mom and dad. The clock on the table glared in bold red numbers, eight o'clock. Groaning, she said, "Four whole hours."

"Well little ones," she said to her tummy.

"By the time I bathe and feed us, we won't have much longer to wait for grandma and grandpa."

Eleven forty-seven, Gabe called her.

"Ms. Wells, your parents and I will be there in ten minutes. Just a quick heads up. See you then."

"Okay, thanks Gabe."

Lola was so happy, she walked to the sitting room and realized there was no food for her parents to eat. Rushing to the kitchen when she smelled the aroma of food, startled, she stopped and held her chest.

"Oh, hello, miss. We're, sorry to startle you. Mr. Hunter called us. He didn't know what your parents liked to eat, so we got a little bit of everything."

Hunter. No wonder I love you so much, she thought, lovingly.

In awe, Lola walked to the large table in amazement. There were all kinds of food. Quickly wiping the tears from her eyes when she heard the door open, she rushed to see her mother and father.

"Mom. Dad," Lola cried, hugging them.

"Honey, it is so good to see you," her mother said with tears in her eyes. "It's been too long."

"Honey, don't hog all the hugs. Save some hugs for her old man," Mr. Wells said, laughing happily wrapping his daughter in his arms.

"Dad, it is so good to see you. I love you both," she continued. She tried to stop the flow of tears, but they continued to flow down her cheeks.

He held her away from him and stared at her stomach. "And what do we have here?"

Standing a little away from them, she smiled as she massaged her stomach.

"Well, in about four months you two are becoming grandparents. Hunter and I are having a baby."

Is it my imagination, or did my dad's entire countenance change?

He quickly hid his discomfort with a huge smile on his face.

"Honey, did you hear our daughter? We are going to be grandparents?"

For the first since she came into this world her mother appeared to have a sadness to her she had never seen before.

"Honey? Did you hear our daughter? We are going to be grandparents."

"Yes. Of course I heard," her mother said, smiling happily. "Lola that is wonderful news. Congratulations."

When her mother hugged her, there was a stiffness to her body that was not there when she hugged her before, Lola thought.

"I know you two must be tired from the trip. Let me show you to your room."

"Honey, we are a little tired, but first, we'd like to know why you are at this place? You have a beautiful home in the best part of town. Why here?" Mr. Wells asked.

Lola didn't quite know how much to tell her parents, but something was not right. Her mother seemed sad all of a sudden and her father was not his jovial self.

"Well it would appear that someone doesn't like me so much. This is called a safe house and I have to be here for a while until Hunter finds out who wants to hurt me."

"What?" Her mother asked, voice raised in fear.

"Lola, baby, you need to come home and live with us. I mean, your father and I will take care of you and the babies. My God," she exclaimed. "Why didn't you come to us in the first place? We are your parents…"

"Mom, please stop. This is the best place for me and the babies to be for now."

"Did you say…babies?"

"Yes. Hunter and I are having twins."

"That's it," her mother said in a commanding tone.

"You are coming home with us."

"And who is this Hunter you keep talking about?"

"Dad, Hunter is the father of our babies. We love each other and we are going to get married when all this dangerous stuff blows over."

"Stuff," her mother almost shouted.

"You call having to stay at a safe house stuff?"

"Momma, please let me show you to your room. We will talk later," Lola said.

All of a sudden she was very tired. Explaining to her mother and father were taking its toll on her.

In their room, Mrs. Wells pulled her husband to the bed, sat down and whispered, "Do you think that crazy ex of mine has something to do with this? I knew something was off, I just couldn't put my hand on it."

Hedging, James said, "I don't see why. I mean, he has not been in our lives since he left you. He doesn't even know that Lola is alive. He thinks you aborted Lola as a baby. I really think you and Lola are overthinking this. A man that did to you what he did shouldn't want to show his face. It is a shame the way he just up and left you with a baby. Not knowing how you were going to make it. His own flesh and blood. I tell you, baby he was just no good from the start. He is probably dead by now."

Rubbing his hands up and down her arms, he smiled.

"I don't want you or Lola to worry about this. I will have my guy ask around and see if he can find out anything."

He looked her in the eyes and said, "I have been taking care of you and Lola ever since I met you and I am not about to stop now. I have loved you since I first laid eyes on you. Our baby girl, Lola, was just icing on the cake. I love her like she is my own daughter. Just try not to worry. I will take care of everything."

"James, why are you so good to me?" She asked, kissing him. "You raised our child, no questions asked.

You…" Ginger stopped and put her hand to her mouth.

"Ginger. Honey. What is it?"

"Do you think Kailani knows I did not abort Lola as a baby and he wants to harm her now? Oh, James," she cried, "I could not stand it if he hurt my baby girl. Especially now that she is having our grandchildren."

"Honey, I asked you not to worry. Haven't I always taken care of you and Lola? Given her the best education. Loved her unconditionally. Now, I don't want you to worry. It will only cause Lola to worry if she knows you are worrying and you know she can't worry. Especially since, as you say, she is having our grandchildren."

Ginger hugged James tightly. "How did I ever get to be so lucky? I love you, James."

"I love you too, honey. Always have. Always will. When I first laid eyes on you, you were the most beautiful woman I had ever seen. There is only one other woman who comes close to your beauty and that is our daughter," James said, kissing her on the cheek.

"Let me check around with some guys I know. Believe me, we will get to the bottom of this."

"Okay."

"Why don't you go and check on Lola and the babies. Make sure she is feeling better."

At the door she turned, smiled and said lovingly, "You are a good man, James. Thank God you saw me the day I was to abort our daughter. I always thought fate had you waiting for me on that street. Now I know it. I don't know what I would have done without you all these years."

"Thank you, honey."

James walked to the door and peeped out to make sure Ginger was gone. Closing the door, he walked to the bed and dialed a number.

"Yeah?" The man said menacingly.

"I need you to get to Hawaii as quickly as you can. Find Mr. Kailani Hamm and kill him. Do you still have that picture of him I sent you?"

"Yes."

"You have a week to get the job done. Money has been transferred to your account. This man cannot get off that island…alive."

"Count it as done."

"Call me when it's done."

James sat on the bed for seconds, smiling deviously, took a deep breath and stood. Closing the door behind him, he walked down the hall.

"Honey, where are you and my daughter? I suddenly have a huge appetite."

"Who is responsible for this wonderful meal?" Ginger asked.

"This roast beef just melts in my mouth and I have never had potatoes this good."

Ginger looked at her daughter and smiled.

"And I pride myself on being a good cook."

"You are a good cook, mom. Hunter had this food catered in."

"By the way, where is this young man you speak of so highly?" James said, putting a portion of the succulent roast beef in his mouth.

"I want to meet this man. Actually, baby girl, I am a little surprised at your behavior. You used to be so prim and proper. Looking down on your friends who did such things. Now you have allowed a man to pump you with those babies before marriage. I never thought I would see the day that our little girl would let a man touch her before marriage."

Ginger quickly glanced at her daughter who was about to cry at the insult.

"James, what a mean thing to say. She told you they are going to get married. Why would you say such a thing?"

"I know and you are right, honey. Lola, daddy is very sorry. I guess I am upset that you did not come to us sooner about your danger. I think I am a little jealous that someone is taking my place in your life. You always have been my little girl. I was out of line and daddy is very sorry."

Lola pushed her seat back and stood up from the table.

"Please excuse me. I seem to have lost my appetite. Hunter did not pump me with these babies, dad. We made love and these babies are a product of that love. Your little girl grew up. Hunter is my lover. You are my dad. Right?"

"And to set the record straight, I never looked down on anyone. And, furthermore, I mean as a dad, you can never pump me up with babies, so Hunter can never take your place. Please don't get it confused. Right, DAD?"

"James, how could you?" Ginger asked once Lola left the room.

"I said I was sorry, Ginger. I don't know what came over me. I guess I am just tired and need some rest. You think I need to apologize again…cause' I am very sorry. I would never hurt Lola. You know that."

"I know. You have been nothing but loving to the both of us. But, please be careful. She is pregnant and her hormones are all over the place."

"I know, honey. Why don't you go and check on her. I will be up later."

Minutes later, James was walking down the hall and heard his wife and Lola talking. Wanting to apologize again, he was about to knock to warn them he was coming in when he heard the word Hawaii.

"Why would Mr. Hunter want to go to Hawaii? He should be here with you. You said you are in danger. Lola, baby, I don't like any of this."

Lola held her mother's hand and said, "Mom, I know dad is not my biological dad."

Ginger put her hand over her mouth and stared at Lola. Her eyes filled with tears. "How long have you known?"

"Long enough. Mom, how could you? I love dad. Although he appears to have changed a little since the last time I saw him, he has taken care of me all my life. I would have understood. That is why Hunter is not here. He is in Hawaii. To see my real dad."

James rushed to his room and dialed a number. "Yeah?"

"Change of plans. I need you in Hawaii now. If you can kill Mr. Hamm by today's end there will be an extra ten thousand dollars waiting for you. Mr. Hamm has to die today."

"I don't really care about the answer, but why the change? Why the rush?"

"You don't really need to know that. Just get the job done today."

"Who are you talking to babe?" Ginger asked.

"Get what job done today?"

"I was just trying to get some information. I will be glad when all this is over. I truly hurt my daughter and I am very sorry. I wish she would come home with us. I think I will go have a talk with her. I love her and did not mean to hurt her."

"I know you didn't, but leave her be for now. She is waiting for a call from Hunter and I finally got her to take a nap. You can talk with her later."

Wrapping her arms around his waist, she smiled and said, "Why don't we take a nap or…"

"Or what?" He asked, knowing what she wanted.

"You know," Ginger smiled seductively, pressing into him.

"Oh, Ginger, baby," he moaned.

"You are my weakness. I love you. Always have and I always will and no one is going to take you away from me."

Ginger looked up at him with concern.

"Of course no one is going to take me away from you. You are my knight in shining armor."

Kissing him sensually, she led him to the bed.

Thirty minutes later, she whispered, "Goodness, James. What got into you, baby? You haven't been that powerful and fierce in a while. I think I saw the stars and the moon."

Caressing his chest, she said contently, "If it's those power drinks you drink all the time, please don't stop. You were a force to be reckoned with."

"I just love you, Ginger. Very much. I never want what we have to end."

"It won't, honey," she sighed sleepily.

"We have to talk about you and Lola. Honey, she knows you are not her biological father."

"How long has she known?" He asked.

"She didn't say. Just that she knows. She also knows who her biological father is. I wanted to ask more questions, but she was still very upset and didn't want to talk about it anymore. I told her to get some rest while she waited on Hunter's phone call."

"I did not know I could hate a man the way I hate Kailani. He destroyed me years ago and he is trying to do it again, but I won't let him. Oh, James. I know it is him who is trying to hurt our Lola. I just know it."

"Calm down, baby. I told you. I will handle it. Just trust me. Okay?" He asked, kissing her gently.

"Okay," she sighed, snuggling up to James.

"You are still my knight-in-shining armor, you do know that don't you? I am supposed to be wide awake, but your good loving has knocked me out."

"Get some rest, baby."

James had a bad feeling that what he had with the woman in his arms might come to a horrible end. Ginger was his life and he wasn't about to give up what they have. He had never been able to tell her no when she wanted to make love. Even now in all this turmoil, she had managed to bring him to total satisfaction. Jaw set, mind made up, when Ginger was sound asleep, he eased from the bed.

I am not giving up what we just shared, have shared for thirty years, to no one. Not even her precious daughter. Damn them grandbabies. Ginger is mine, his mind raged.

"Is it done?" He whispered after he walked in the bathroom and shut the door.

"Not yet. There was a man with him and they left his office in a rush, but I am on it now. I really need to stay focused. I will call you when it is done."

Hawaii

"Mr. Hamm? Kailani Hamm?"

"Yes? Who is this?"

"I need to speak with you, Mr. Hamm. It is very urgent."

"I'm sorry, but I don't know you. Who is this? You have two seconds before I hang…"

"It's about Ms. Wells. Ginger Wells. Hall I believe was her maiden name before she got married."

There was a long pause at the other end of the line.

"Meet me at Hamm Technologies. Do you have the address?"

"Yes."

Forty minutes later Hunter parked across the street and stared at the building that had the name Hamm's Technology in bold gray letters.

"I am here," Hunter spoke into his microphone. "Stay focused and keep a sharp eye." Stepping from the car he walked across the street and into the building.

"Sir, Mr. Hunter is here,"

"Show him in, Mandy. Thank you."

"Mr. Hunter. Have a seat."

"Thank you."

Hunter looked around the office. It was huge, but not overly decorated. His eyes stopped when they got to Mr. Hamm's desk. There was no mistaking the picture of a beautiful woman staring up at Mr. Hamm. You could see the love in their eyes for each other. Another photo, the woman was standing against a tree with shorts on with hair blowing in the wind.

There was another woman who had the same stunning looks and she was carrying his twin babies. The thought of Lola caused electricity to go through his body. He would be glad when he could hold her in his arms again.

Mr. Hamm saw Hunter looking at the pictures and he slowly turned the photos face down on the desktop.

"Mr. Hunter, you wanted to talk with me about Ginger? Ms. Hall?"

"How well did you know Mrs. Wells?"

"I would prefer if you didn't call her Mrs. Wells in my presence. She is still Ms. Hall to me."

Kailani paused and got up from his chair and walked to the window.

"I knew Ms. Hall very well. We met and fell in love when I came to the states to visit."

"If you loved her, why did you leave her when she told you she was pregnant?"

"That was the biggest mistake of my life. I thought I did not want to be tied down with a child. I left and came back to Hawaii."

"A few days after I got back I was miserable without Ginger. I realized how much I really did love her…and the baby. I wanted them to come here so we could talk, work things out and hopefully get married. I was about to have all the money we needed. To give Ginger everything she wanted and more."

Mr. Hamm put his hands to his face for seconds before he rushed to his desk and took the picture with him and Ginger on it and threw it against the wall.

His secretary rushed into the office. "It's alright, Mandy. Close the door on your way out." She glanced at Hunter and gently closed the door.

Kailani picked up the picture, shook off the glass and walked back to his desk.

"Mr. Wells and I grew up together. We were friends."

He stared at the photo hard before he tore it up and let it fall through his fingers.

"I thought we were closer than blood brothers. I could not leave Hawaii to get my family. I was working on a deal with a billion dollar company. If the company bought my brand, I would have enough money to take care of a wife and baby many times over. I was over the moon with happiness."

"Mr. Wells used to stare at the pictures on my desk whenever he came to my office. Told me how lucky I was to have such a beautiful woman and child on the way. He volunteered to go get my family and bring them over here to me. He knew I could not leave at that time. I gave him the last six thousand dollars I had to bring my family to me."

"A week later he called and told me that Ginger did not want to see me. That she hated me and that she had aborted my baby. I was totally devastated. A part of me died."

Kailani walked over to the side bar and poured a drink and let it slide down his throat in one gulp.

I'm sorry. I forgot my manners. Would you like…"

"No."

Hunter did not like the way this story was going. If what Mr. Hamm was saying had any merit, Lola's danger was closer to home than he realized. He had a few more pieces of the puzzle he needed.

"Mr. Hamm, who is Frank?"

"I don't know. Ginger never said anything about a man named Frank while we dated."

"Why did you pay us so much money to protect your daughter? Who told you that Lola was in danger?"

"That is my business and…"

"I beg to differ, Mr. Hamm."

"And why is that, Mr. Hunter?"

Without waiting for a reply, he jumped up from his chair. "Mr. Hunter, you need to leave."

"You know, Mr. Hamm. I have tried to be patient with you. Lola, your daughter, is carrying my children. Twins. Someone is trying to kill her and I will not rest until I find out what is going on."

Mr. Hamm sat down and stared at the photo of Ginger standing by the tree.

"Lola is pregnant?" He whispered.

"With my grandbabies?"

11

"Yes! And if you are not willing to help me I am wasting my time here with you."

Hunter was at the door about to leave…

"When James, Mr. Wells, did not come back right away. I called him and asked what was taking so long. I wanted my family here with me. I wanted to see Ginger's stomach grow big with my child. He told me that Ginger had gotten rid of the baby and that she hated me and never wanted to see me again."

"And you just took his word at face value? No questions. Nothing?"

"I told you," Kailani said, frustrated.

"We were brothers…or so I thought. I thought I could trust him. I told him to keep a thousand dollars of the money I gave him for going to get my family and to give the rest to Ginger. She might need it to help out in some way."

"I was crushed. The light went out in my life and it has never burned as bright. Two months had gone by and although I now had money, it meant nothing if I could not share it with my Ginger."

"I called James trying to get more information, and when he finally answered, he told me that he had moved on to Washington. I never questioned him because he once told me that he loved Washington and wanted to live there one day. He thanked me for the thousand dollars… said it helped him move to Washington."

"My love for Ginger only grew. The more I tried to forget her, the more I loved her. I decided to try at least one last time to see her and ask if we could start over. I wanted to apologize for not coming to get her myself and ask for forgiveness. Maybe try for another baby in the future if she would only agree to marry me."

He paused as if the past had caught up with him.

"Mr. Hamm, what happened? Please. Time is of the essence. I need to get back to Lola and my babies."

"Yes. Of course. I am sorry."

He took another drink before he talked again.

"I got to New York and I could barely wait to see my Ginger again. If I could just explain to her what happened. Tell her how sorry I was about us and the baby."

Hunter saw the change in him before he picked up the entire bottle of whiskey and threw it across the room and hit the wall. Hunter waited. He only had one more piece of the puzzle he needed.

"Imagine my surprise when I got to the house where Ginger lived. James and my Ginger were on the couch locked in each other arms and…" He stopped to gather himself.

"The only thing that kept me from killing them both was the smile on her face. She appeared happy. She had forgotten me. It had only been months since I left and already she had forgotten me in the arms of another man. My best friend. I realized at that time that James had lied to me and probably my Ginger as well."

"Why in God's name did you not call him out on it?"

"Ginger seemed happy. If she was happy I didn't want to see the light go out of her beautiful eyes. Besides, James had told me that she never wanted to see me again and that she hated me. She had aborted my baby…or so I thought."

"You mean to tell me that all these years you let your best friend get away with stealing your woman? Who was carrying your baby? My God, man, Mr. Wells stole your family and you did nothing about it."

"I didn't know at the time that she was still pregnant with my baby. I thought she had aborted it. He said she hated me. I did not want the eyes that had looked at me with so much love and adoration look at me now with hatred."

"If they had laughed at me because I was there, I just might have shot them both. A broken heart can only take so much. So I left. I was so broken, I barely made it back to the airport. If I had been driving, I probably would have driven off some cliff or drove into an ocean. I wanted to die."

"When I got back to Hawaii, I went insane for a few months. The thought of him touching Ginger drove me mad. "I drowned in booze and work. Everyday. I lost weight. My mom came to live with me to make sure I ate every day. She got on my nerves so badly, I started eating and eased up on my drinking so she could go home. The company grew, but I was more miserable every day."

"What turned it around for you? Obviously, you stopped the drinking. You are sober now."

"Years later. Someone. I don't know who. Called and told me that I had a daughter. That my baby girl was alive. He sent me pictures of her. That did not do much good. I mean, her beauty came from her mother. The only thing that was in my favor was her skin tone and hair texture."

"This person even got strands of her hair and sent it for me to get a DNA test. I would not believe it until I had proof. I could not go down that road again. The thought that it might not be my daughter after all these years tore my insides to shreds. It would have taken me out."

"Fortunately, for me her DNA was a match. I stopped drinking. Got myself together so when we met I did not want her to see her dad as an alcoholic. Today was the first time I had a drink in years."

Hunter knew this was the piece of the puzzle he needed. "Mr. Hamm, who sent you the pictures and the strands of hair?"

"I honestly don't know. I still have the letter that he sent me. The man said something about how he was promised his daughter when he grew up if he helped him. Then he said something about how the man lied to him and his brother."

"Do you still have the letter? I need to see it. Now!"

"Yes, I have it, but it is at my house."

"Can we go there now? Lola and her mother are in grave danger and I think I know who is behind all of this madness."

They rushed from the office.

"Mandy, you can leave for today."

Before she could say thank you, he was gone.

In the car Hunter quickly called his men.

"Hey, boss. Did you find out anythi…"

"Gabe, lock it down. We have been compromised. No one gets out. No one, Gabe."

"Bear is locking it down as we speak."

"I need you to get Lola and her mother away from Mr. Wells. If you can't get Mrs. Wells from her husband, get Lola to safety. You hear me, Gabe?"

"I hear you, boss."

"Someone is going to be on the grounds outside that should not be there. Be ready for him. Frank had a brother. A twin. He may be dangerous, but try not to kill him. I need him alive."

"Nick?"

"I'm here."

"Watch your back. Meet me and Mr. Hamm at his home." Hunter gave Nick the address.

"Good morning, baby," James said, reaching for his wife. To his surprise, she was not in bed. Thinking she was in the shower, he went in search of her in the bathroom.

"Hmm," he said.

Slipping on some pants and a shirt, he quickly walked down the hall. Gently tapping on Lola's bedroom door, he got no answer.

His wife's laughter was coming from the dining room. Smiling, he walked down the stairs.

"Good morning to my favorite ladies. Did everyone sleep well?" He walked over to his wife and whispered, "I know you slept well, my dear."

Ginger blushed and looked over to her daughter.

"It's okay, mom," she said smiling.

"I've seen dad kiss you before. I almost caught y'all a few times when you were doing a little more than kissing."

Her fifty year old mother was blushing so badly, Lola started laughing and could barely stop.

"Mom, you are hilarious. Blushing at fifty."

James looked from Ginger to Lola. The two most important women in his life. Their laughter caused his heart to swell with love. At least Ginger did."

And now he was to become a grandparent to twins.

Oh, well, he thought. *For Ginger's love I can bare her daughter for a while longer. Life couldn't get any better*, he thought.

Sometimes I wonder what life would have been like if there had not been a baby to contend with. No baby to come between me and Ginger, James thought.

A thought he had pondered many times over. He checked his phone. There was no text that the job was done.

What is taking him so long to get the job done? He ranted in his mind. It was morning. *I should have gotten word that Mr. Hamm was sleeping with the fishes by now.*

Suddenly, James got up from the table.

"Honey, where are you going? You should eat while the food is hot."

"I need to make a quick phone call. I promise I will be right back. Please excuse me."

"What is taking so long?" He asked, minutes later. "The job should have been done by now."

"Why is what taking so long? Is that you, Mr. Wells? What job?"

Heart beating frantically, he immediately swiped off his phone.

"You sleazy, no good for nothing," James said under his breath.

"How in hell did you manage to get caught? You couldn't go to Hawaii and do one little job. Stupid imbecile. No one is taking my Ginger away…and I am not going to jail," he whispered.

He knew the man he hired was going to talk. Tell everything just to save his own neck. Rushing back to the dining room, trying to play it cool, he looked at Ginger.

"Honey, we need to leave."

"But why? We just got here yesterday. What's wrong?"

"Let's go. Now, Ginger!" He exclaimed.

"I will explain it all later, but we have to leave now."

"Lola. I'm sorry, sweet heart, but we will come again…" Ginger was saying when James came and pulled her from the chair.

"Now, Ginger," James almost shouted.

"James, take it easy. I just need to go and pack my things."

"Forget your things. We need to leave now."

Reaching for her hand he was pulling her to the door.

"Dad. Wait. What is going on?" Lola said, getting up from her chair.

"Let mom go. Don't treat her like that. You go and take care of whatever you have to take care of and let mom stay here with me."

"No! She is coming with me," James said, opening the door forcefully, but stopped immediately.

"Hello, James."

"Kailani," James said, smiling deceitfully.

"Man, but it is good to see you."

Not paying him no mind, Kailani glanced at Ginger.

"My God!" He exclaimed, softly.

"Thirty years," he said in wonder.

"Hello, Ginger," Kailani said, barely breathing.

"It's been a long time, but you are still as beautiful as ever."

James looked from Ginger to Kailani. What he saw in her eyes was not hatred, but a look he thought never to see in them.

Have I meant nothing to her all these years? His mind raged.

"Don't talk to her. She doesn't belong to you. She belongs to me. She hates you, remember? She can't stand you. You left her to fend for herself and the child you abandoned."

Eyes never leaving hers, "Did I abandon her, James? Or did you steal her from me?" Kailani asked.

Laughing unsteadily, James tried walking over to his wife, but a man James did not know blocked his way.

"That's far enough, Mr. Wells," Gabe said.

"And who the hell are you? Get out of my way. My wife and I were just leaving. Honey, let's go," he said desperately.

<h1 style="text-align:center">12</h1>

"James, what did he mean when he said that you stole me from him?"

"Ginger, I said let's go. This man is very dangerous. He was coming back to New York to kill you and the baby, so I asked him if I could come in his stead."

Kailani tried to get to James to beat the truth out of him. "Why you lying no good for nothing. I can kill you for lying to Ginger. You took my life away. Without Ginger and my baby I barely wanted to live. You were supposed to be my friend."

Hunter stopped him before he could get to James. Breathing heavily, Hunter held him until he calmed down.

"I'm okay," Kailani continued to breathe heavily, all the while keeping his eyes on James.

"You stabbed me in the back in the worst possible way. You told me Ginger had aborted the baby. That she hated my guts and never wanted to see me again." Heaving a heavy sigh, Kailani appeared to have lost all fight.

"I just want to know one thing. What did you do with the six thousand dollars I gave you to bring Ginger and my baby she was carrying over to Hawaii so we could talk things out, get married and raise our baby together?"

"Get married?" Ginger exclaimed.

"James told me that you hated me. Never wanted to see me again. That I needed to abort the baby because you never wanted to see me or the baby again. That you had made a mistake dating a black woman."

Kailani turned to Ginger.

"I did not see color when I was with you. I honestly loved you with all my heart. The biggest mistake I ever made was when I left you and my baby behind. I couldn't come at the time to get you, so James volunteered. I gave him all the money that I had to bring my family to me."

He turned to James.

"I trusted you, man. When you told me that Ginger had aborted my baby, I told you to give Ginger five thousand dollars and for you to keep a thousand to help you with your move to Washington."

"Lies. All lies I tell you. I don't know what he is talking about," James said, cursing.

He started toward Ginger, but Hunter stopped him. Hunter looked to Lola to make sure she was okay. Lola held her mother's hand tightly and whispered she was okay.

"Ginger, baby, let's go. No wonder you hate him so much. The man is a liar and is no good."

He reached for her, but she hung back. Ginger had long sat down. Her legs had given out on her a while back. The more she heard, the weaker they had gotten.

"Is that true?" She asked James, but knew the answer already.

"Of course, it's not true. I told you, the man is a liar. Now let's go. I don't want to leave you here, but I will if you continue to listen to all this foolishness."

"You never gave me any money from Kai. You told me Kai said, and I quote, "Kailani said that you could starve for all he cared." End quote."

Ginger was so heartbroken, she couldn't move. She looked at James. The man who had been her knight in shining armor. Her lover. The man who had taken care of her all these years. Had loved her devotedly. Raised their daughter as his own. All these years had been built on lies.

"Why? James, why?"

"Honey, there is no why. I love you. I love Lola as my own."

"Then why did you pay me to kill Lola after your man was to kill Mr. Hamm? Did you ever tell your wife that you always hated her daughter? That you only put up with her because you loved her mother so much you would have done anything to keep her," Frances, Frank's brother said.

"Shut up," James shouted, unraveling. "I don't know this man I tell you."

Frances continued.

"How you wanted Mrs. Wells all to yourself? How you pitted Franklin and I against each other. You son of a bitch," he grated.

"You promised me that if I helped you get rid of Mr. Hamm, just in case your assassin didn't come through, Lola would be mine. But, you also promised Lola to Franklin. And when Franklin died, you tried to have me killed."

"You are sick in the head. I don't know you. What? Did Mr. Hamm pay you to say all this so he can tear my wife and me apart?" James said viciously.

Hunter pressed play on his phone.

"James. What do I owe the pleasure?" Frances asked.

"Now that your brother is dead. Lola will definitely be yours. All you have to do is take her far away from her mother or if you don't want her then just kill her. Her father has been a thorn in my side for nearly thirty-one years. There will be no need to kill Lola if you just take her away from here and her mother."

Hunter pressed the fast forward button on his phone and pressed play again.

"Lola and her friend will be at the peer. Take them hot out for all I care. Make it look like an accident," James continued.

"No. No. No," Ginger cried in total shock and dismay. Lola clung to her mother trying to comfort her.

"I think that will get you enough time in prison for somebody to latch on to that body of yours," Hunter said, walking to cuff him and turn him over to the authorities.

"You paid my own brother to kill me, you son of a bitch," Frances grated through clenched teeth.

Frances turned to Lola.

"I finally realized you were not in love with me when I saw you and Mr. Hunter together. Mr. Wells said that you loved me, but didn't know how to tell me. He fed my twin brother the same crock of lies, but Franklin couldn't let it go. He hung on James' every word."

"I came to the hospital to talk with you, but I scared you instead. I am truly sorry for the misery my brother and I caused you. It was James…"

"Shut up," James shouted, breathing madly.

"Lies. It's all lies. Don't believe him, Ginger."

Frances started towards James.

"Don't come any further," James said, pulling a weapon from his pants.

"Nobody moves or I take Lola out first."

He looked at Lola with hatred.

"You just wouldn't die would you? I hated the fact that your mother would not abort you. I once tripped her hoping if she fell on her stomach, she would lose you. But no. The doctor said you would live. I had to pretend all these years that I loved you. It was supposed to be just Ginger and me."

"No. No. No," Ginger continued in abject misery, shaking her head trying to rid her mind of the total betrayal she had lived for thirty years. She clung to her daughter for life.

Hunter tried to ease towards Lola, but James stopped him. "Don't you move another step," James sniveled. "But, I do want your phone with that recording on it."

Hunter gave the phone to James.

"Why did you do that? We needed that evidence so he can go to jail for what he did," Frances yelled.

James finally turned and stared at Frances.

"I always did think you had more sense than Franklin. I hated that they killed him. He always did my bidding with no questions asked, but you always were better at thinking. Your only weakness was your love for Lola."

Before anyone knew what was happening, James pulled the trigger. The blast was deafening. Lola and Ginger screamed in terror.

Turning the gun on Lola, he shouted, "You came between Ginger and me. You had to go and get pregnant…with twins. Taking more of your mother's love from me. I hate you Lola, you bitch. I hate you."

Thinking only of keeping Lola and Ginger safe, Hunter ran to James, but not quick enough. Aiming at Lola, he pulled the trigger.

"Noooo!" Shouted Kailani, running to cover his daughter and Ginger.

Hunter wrestled James to the floor, but not before he got off one round.

"Did I get her?" He asked, laughing viciously.

"Did I get that bitch? I don't care if I go to jail as long as I killed her and them babies."

Hunter hit James hard across the face.

"Those are my babies and my fiancé you are talking about and I don't take kindly to that."

Hunter's men came and put the cuffs on James.

"I love you, Ginger, baby," he continued to say until he was out of ear range.

"That stupid buffoon, Hamm didn't deserve you. I made you happy for thirty years. Don't let them do this to us, Ginger."

One of Hunter's guys checked on Frances. After he checked for a pulse, he turned to Hunter, He is breathing, but barely. We need an ambulance and fast."

"Lola, baby are you alright?" Ginger asked.

"Yes. I am fine. It's Mr. Hamm, my dad. He's on the floor, mom and he is not moving."

They both rushed to Kailani.

"Kai," she called him for short, "are you alright? Can you hear me?" Ginger asked, kneeling by his side.

"Dad. We are here for you, dad. Please don't die," Lola whispered in his ear.

EPILOGUE

"Honey, take it easy," Hunter said to Lola.

"Don't overdo it."

"Okay. I won't. I just want everything to be perfect when our parents get here."

"Come here."

Lola walked into his arms. Holding her close he started talking.

"Honey, as far as I am concerned, everything is perfect. We have two beautiful babies. We have each other's love. We have the love of family. My parents, and your parents are over the moon with the grandbabies and my sister still teases me about going online for a date. She wants to take all the credit for bringing us together."

"Hunter, baby, she can take all the credit so long as I get to keep you."

She looked up from his shoulders and smiled lovingly. "You are a keeper."

"Thank you," he said, kissing her on the forehead.

"Are you okay with your parents? I mean thirty years is a long time for them to have been apart."

"Yes. I'm okay with them getting back together. I mean, it was a hard and rough road at first, but I think mom is truly happy with dad. At first, I didn't like the fact that she was leaving me to live in Hawaii, but dad convinced me how much he loved her, even now."

"Can you imagine not marrying anyone after he thought mom didn't want him? Because of the love in his heart for her he told her the past was meant to stay in the past."

"Yes, Lola. Baby, I can imagine the love your father has for your mother because of the love I feel for you. I fell hard for you. I don't even want to think about life without you and my babies."

"Thank you, sweetheart. Loving you the way I do, I understand my dad better. He asked me to trust him that he would take care of momma. So yes. I'm okay. I'm really kinda glad daddy was shot."

"Why?"

"Well, if daddy had not gotten shot, I think momma would have lost it. Gone completely mad because of what dad, I mean James did to her."

"One day I really thought she was going to pull out all her hair. She screamed and fell to the floor and cried her eyes out. Daddy. The man I thought was my dad hurt momma very badly."

"She had loved him for thirty years. Hung on his every word. Gave herself to him in total submission.

She never questioned his lies about what he told her about my real dad. Not one time. The guilt was tearing her apart."

"She went through the house and started throwing everything James ever bought her or she thought he bought and started breaking it. She was throwing small furniture into the wall. Trashing the place. When she saw the fear in my eyes, she said she was sorry, fell to the floor and cried some more."

"Going to the hospital every day. Talking with Mr. Hamm, my dad, and getting the real story and knowing that he forgave her for everything, she got better and better every day. Mr. Hamm telling her that through it all he still loved her, helped to make her a stronger woman."

"Do you ever think about James?"

"Sometimes. I mean, I called him daddy for thirty years. He kept his animosity for me hidden very well. He was the only dad I knew. I don't hate him for what he did. I am too happy to hate."

"My heart is filled with too much love to hate. My family means the world to me. You. The twins. Our little one. Your parents. Your sister, and my parents. The guys…your team. My heart does not have room to hate."

"Remember when we went to the prison to see him?"

"I remember," Hunter said.

"I asked him why he hated me so much."

"He said because I reminded him of my real father. He was angry because I was not his daughter and to look at me, it reminded him of my real dad."

"He said he didn't like the fact that Mr. Hamm had given momma a baby and she would not have one for him. Whenever he asked her to give him a child, she would flat out refuse. Instead of taking his anger out on momma, he would look at me and hate me."

"He then looked at me and sneered wickedly. By that time I was furious and gave him a piece of my mind."

"You know what, *daddy dear*? Frances was right. You are so pathetic. You blame everyone for your own dirty, nasty evil ways. You took another man's family for thirty years. You had people killed to cover up your evil deeds, and yet you are not repentant. I gave him one final look and said, I hope you rot in here."

"His head went back as if I had slapped him. When I got up to leave his entire countenance changed as if he had a split personality."

"He looked me straight in the eyes and said, "You are the reason I got twenty-five years to life in this hell hole. Get out of my sight and never come back.""

"That's why you had that nightmare the first night after you talked with him?"

"Yes."

"Well, baby. All of that is in the past now, thank God. I am just so happy that we came through it all okay."

He paused, gently rubbing her back.

"At least Frances will have a chance at life. Testifying against James helped his case. The only thing he was truly guilty of was the fact that he withheld evidence about his brother and James," Lola said.

"Yeah, but I do understand why he got six months in jail and three years' probation," Hunter explained.

"If he had come forward with what he knew on his brother, it might have saved a life."

Resting her head on his shoulder.

"I am so happy the Lord gave me you. I love you, Hunter Nichols."

"Wow. Thank you, baby?"

"You are very welcome."

"Would you give me another baby if I wanted another one from you? I mean not now, but maybe later. I kinda understand why your mother didn't want to have another one, but…" Lola stopped his flow of words with a kiss.

Seconds went by before she answered, "You already have."

Holding her at arm's length, he looked at her lovingly, "You are?"

"Yes. I am pregnant."

Hunter enclosed her in his arms lovingly.

"Honey, I'm sorry. I didn't mean give me one now. Don't you think the twins are too young…?"

Lola put two fingers to his lips to stop his flow of words.

"First, Mr. Nichols, you are the one who gave me this baby. Second, the twins are not too young as long as we continue to give them the love they need. And, I think we have enough love to go around."

"Don't ever be sorry for leaving a part of your love with me after the loving is over."

Holding him close to her heart, caressing the back of his neck, she whispered, "Hunter, baby you love me so good. How could I not want the child you leave with me after the loving is over? I want this baby and more so long as you are the man that leaves them in my body."

"Oh, Lola," Hunter groaned.

"You make the hairs stand up straight on my head. I love you. I love you, baby. Are we really going to have another baby?"

"Yes. I don't know why you are so surprised. You are so strong. So forceful. So brilliant. So all-consuming with your loving, how could I not get pregnant? Hunter, baby. How could I not. You are real, Hunter. A real man."

He began kissing Lola so thoroughly, weakly she clung to him. Kissing him back with such ardor, he whispered, "Can you give me five minutes?"

"For what?" She sighed, knowingly.

"I can show you better."

"Take all the time you need," Lola sighed, kissing the man she loved senseless.

"Oh, Hunter," she sighed in his mouth,

"Please, take all the time you need."

"Was that long enough for you tiger," Lola asked, purring from contentment.

Hunter turned and looked at her.

"I love you, woman. I honestly see why you are pregnant. I have nothing but love to give you, baby."

"So long as it is me and only me, you give your love to, I am available every day."

"Thank you sweetheart. Please, just don't ever stop loving and needing me."

"Okay. I won't."

Laying her head back on his shoulder, she asked, "Hunter?"

"Yes?"

"Do you ever think about leaving the guys and the business? Do you miss it?"

Without hesitation, "No. I never want to put my family in danger. It paid very well, but I love you and my babies more. Much, much more. I still work for the government part time as well as a few more projects I'm working on."

"I also tried to give Mr. Hamm his money back, but you would think I asked him to jump off Mount Rushmore to his death. He really loves you, baby."

"I know. He saved my life when he jumped in front of me and took the bullet that was meant for me."

"If you ever need help with money, since you left the business, I have money saved. What's mine is now ours."

Hunter stared at Lola in wonder before he began kissing Lola senseless. The love she had for him showed in everything she did for him. Now she wanted to share her finances.

"Why, Hunter," she sighed helplessly. "You need five more minutes."

"Oh, baby," he whispered.

"A lifetime won't be enough. Thank you for the offer, but I have enough money to last us a lifetime. But, Lola. Baby, money can't buy what you're making me feel right now. Money can't buy the love I feel for you. The respect you have for me."

Satiated from Hunter's powerful loving, Lola eventually eased from her husband's arms, and turned to walk away. "Leaving so soon?"

"Hunter, baby if I had stayed in your strong arms, I would have had my way with you…again, in front of our nosy babies." Lola started laughing.

"Look at them, Hunter. They are staring at us in wonder."

"I am looking at them, but what you said about having your way with me is what stuck in my mind."

Easing from the bed, walking towards her with that look in his eyes, he stopped when his phone chimed.

"You will have to do a raincheck on having your way with me…again. That was your dad. They are on their way."

She was getting nervous and happy at the same time as she rushed to take a quick shower.

He grabbed her hand as she passed him.

"Take it easy, baby. It is your parents and you know they love you."

"I know. It's just that I have not seen momma since I had the twins. And that was a year ago. She and dad stayed a while, but do you think momma is happy in Hawaii? Really happy with dad. They had a lot of hurdles to jump before things righted itself. I know momma was a little mentally challenged for a while because James hurt her so badly, but dad's love and patience helped to heal her heart."

"When they get here, pay very close attention to your mother. You will be able to tell if she is happy or not. It will be hard to hide."

"Okay," she said, rushing to the shower.

He looked at his twins who was looking at him for attention. He stooped down in front of them.

"How are my babies doing? Daddy loves you so much," he said, kissing them both, laughing at the joy they showed from his attention.

He checked to make sure they were secure in their swings and turned the music box on so it would keep them company before taking a quick shower in the bath down the hall from them. He had finished his shower and changed when Lola came downstairs. She was a sight to behold.

"Lola. Sweetheart. You look absolutely lovely?"

"Thank you, baby. I don't think I have to tell you how handsome you look. I'm sure all the women do that every day. Cause' Hunter, baby, you are a very handsome, well put together man."

"The only woman who says it that matters is you."

Lola was reaching up to accept the kiss Hunter was about to give her when tired of being ignored, the twins, a boy and a girl, started chanting, and knocking their rattles against the swings. "Da da da da."

Hunter looked at Lola and burst out laughing.

"Baby, don't look at me like that. I think I heard a ma, ma the other day."

"Yeah right," she said.

"I carried them for nine months. The little boogers. Birthed them through pain that was atrocious, and the little darlings says da, da all the time."

Smiling as she walked over to the swings, she stooped down and started talking gibberish to her darlings.

"You can say da, da, any time you want my little ones. After all he is the one that gave you to me and I love da da very much. Yes I do."

They started kicking their legs and swinging their little arms all over the place in joy.

"You are going to have a little brother or sister in the near future. Yes you are," she said happily.

Hunter stared at his family with love and pride. *Lord, it hasn't been easy this past year*, he thought. *But by your grace Lord, we are doing just fine.*

He looked at his little girl and already she was a beauty like her mother and grandmother. His son, thank God, was the spitting image of him. Pride was flowing through his veins just to look at the beautiful babies they had produced.

God, you are good, he thought. His phone chimed again.

Swiping his phone off, he looked at Lola.

"That was my parents. They will be here in fifteen minutes. My sister and her husband. Pam, and her husband, the guys and their families are not far behind."

He looked at her, winked, smiled and add, "I also invited Anna and Sam."

Trying hard to keep the tears from her eyes, Lola looked at Hunter in appreciation.

"No wonder I love you so much. You are a very good man, Hunter. You are going to get a thank you so big tonight from me."

"And you are going to get a big surprise tonight as well. A big, big surprise."

The look on his wife's face was priceless. Hunter's laugh did her heart good.

"Remember, baby, that I love you and no one comes before you, the baby you are carrying, and those twins. We have help with the food and all the preparations, so don't overdo it."

"I won't, baby. Should we tell our families that we're having another baby?"

"Can we just enjoy this moment to ourselves for a few months? Let them lavish the twins with all that love for now. The little one will have our love until you start to show," Hunter said, lovingly.

"Hold me, Hunter," Lola whispered.

Wrapping her in his arms, he asked, "Is everything alright?"

"Yes. Everything is more than alright. That's just it, Hunter. I feel so blessed and I thank God for that. I know all on-line dates don't turn out this wonderful.

Anna's on-line date was the date from hell…horrible. But, you, Hunter. Of all the men on that website, God blessed me with one of his best."

"Lola, baby," he said, holding her close, kissing her thoroughly.

"You can't talk like that when all the family will be here in minutes. Baby you have me wanting to make love to you all the time."

He wiped her cheeks with his finger as the tears of thankfulness continued to fall.

"I know how you feel, sweetheart. I went on that dating site as a dare to my sister, and found the love of my life. I know it was a higher power that brought us together. Let's try and get through today with our families and tonight we can show each other how truly grateful we are to have each other."

Ten minutes later, the doorbell rang. Hunter and Lola, hand in hand, walked to open the door to nothing but love. The love of family.

Hunter opened the door and the look on Lola's mother's face told it all. Lola had never seen her mother this happy before in all of her years. Her smile. Her body language. Her eyes were glowing. And her dad looked better than ever. He looked at least ten years younger. When he looked to Ginger to enter the door before him, the love in his eyes was pure bliss.

"Any more doubt? Or questions about your mother and father being happy?" He whispered under his breath after he closed the door.

Her mother and father went straight to the twins. Taking them from the swings.

"Nary a one, my darling," she said contentedly.

"I love you, Lola Nichols," he whispered lovingly. "You, the little one you are carrying, and those twins have my heart." "Touche', my darling," she said, reaching for his hand. "Touché'."

The End

ABOUT THE AUTHOR

Betty Brooks resides in Alabama, and is the proud mother of two, who are the joys of her life. As a hobby, she enjoys writing, reading and sewing. Her interests are singing, songs and movies. Her faith, belief, strength and power come from the known God and his son, Jesus the Christ.

"Happy reading to all who choose this book for enjoyment."

For more information on upcoming books and events, please visit:

https://bettracebooks.wordpress.com/